HELLO KI

Angela S. Choi was born in Hong Kong and now lives in San Francisco. After graduating from Yale, she practiced law until she realised she no longer wanted to live life in six-minute increments, and so took up the pen at the tender age of 30. *Hello Kitty Must Die* is her debut novel.

www.angelaschoi.com

ANGELA S. CHOI

Hello Kitty
Must Die

VINTAGE BOOKS
London

Published by Vintage 2012

2 4 6 8 10 9 7 5 3 1

Copyright © Angela S. Choi 2010

Angela S. Choi has asserted her right under the Copyright, Designs
and Patents Act 1988 to be identified as the author of this work

First published in USA in 2010 by Tyrus Books

Vintage
Random House, 20 Vauxhall Bridge Road,
London SW1V 2SA

www.vintage-books.co.uk

Addresses for companies within The Random House Group Limited
can be found at: www.randomhouse.co.uk/offices.htm

The Random House Group Limited Reg. No. 954009

A CIP catalogue record for this book
is available from the British Library

ISBN 9780099570493

The Random House Group Limited supports The Forest Stewardship
Council (FSC®), the leading international forest certification
organisation. Our books carrying the FSC label are printed on FSC®
certified paper. FSC is the only forest certification scheme endorsed
by the leading environmental organisations, including Greenpeace.
Our paper procurement policy can be found at:
www.randomhouse.co.uk/environment

MIX
Paper from
responsible sources
FSC® C016897

Printed and bound by CPI Group (UK) Ltd, Croydon, CR0 4YY

To Mom, Dad, Meatball, & St. Jude

I would like to thank the wonderful people who made this project possible:

Robert Ressler, my creative writing coach, for guiding me through my transition to the writing life

John Kithas, for employing me while I wrote this book

Lynda, for telling me to just start this book already

Adrian Weber, my friend, personal editor, and reader, for helping me come up with a kickass title, editing my first draft, and cheering me on

Marie Mockett for guiding me through the querying/ publication process

Andrea Somberg for giving me suggestions to polish the novel

Josh Getzler, my fabulous agent, for going above and beyond the call of duty to sell this novel

Alison Janssen, for being a brilliant editor

Ben Leroy, for buying this novel in the first place

Mom & Dad for putting me here on this planet

Meatball, my fat parakeet, for being an inspiration

St. Jude, for prayers answered

Dick Cheney for being Dick Cheney

CHAPTER
ONE

I T ALL STARTED with my missing hymen.

One week before my twenty-eighth birthday, I decided to take my own virginity with a silicone dildo coated in two-percent Lidocaine gel.

Silicone dildos are the best. Firm, smooth, easy to clean, and most importantly, you can boil them in water. We Chinese folks love to boil things. Our chopsticks, our teacups, our pots and pans, and especially our drinking water. Nothing goes inside our bodies without being boiled in water first.

Silicone dildos are also the ideal choice for people who have allergies.

I have a lot of allergies. That and I didn't quite fancy the idea of asking some emergency room doctor to pick glass shards out of my vagina. And as the saleswoman said, glass dildos would be "less than ideal" for my present intentions.

I selected a purple medium-sized dildo with a flared base for easy grip. As it was not attached to a male body, I figured I would need to have a firm handle on it. Not that it would have gone anywhere except out the way it went in, but still.

And like everything else, it was "Made in China." A fact my parents would surely appreciate. They like everything made in the home country.

I named my dildo Mr. Happy. I thought it would be an appropriate name for something that would have the privilege of destroying my family's honor, which I had upheld dutifully between my legs for nearly three decades.

The existence of that untouched membrane sent every American boy running, especially when I told them that we couldn't have sex until we got married. As no one wanted to marry me by the third date, my insistence of keeping my hymen intact put a huge damper on my dating life. Had my parents and I stayed in Hong Kong, it would have been less of a problem. Traditional Chinese people frown upon premarital sex.

But we were not in China. We lived in the home city of the Sisters of Perpetual Indulgence who had been "defining San Francisco values since 1979." We lived in the golden state of California, which had the second highest teen pregnancy rate in the nation. We lived in the United States of America, the nation of *Girls Gone Wild*, where that thin sliver of tissue did not get anyone's family an extra head of cattle. All it did was keep me home every Friday and Saturday night.

So when I met Chip, I decided to assimilate into debauchery and vice, to bite into forbidden fruit American-style. Family honor be damned. Not because Chip was Mr. Right, but because he happened to be Mr. There-At-The-Right-Time. Except there was a problem: my father.

"You're not coming home tonight, Fiona?"

"Big project. Whole office pulling an all-nighter."

"Okay. Work hard."

And I was free to sin.

Thank God the Chinese are not into honor killing—at least I would not be dragged out into the village square and stoned, stabbed, or set on fire. I considered myself lucky.

It would just make my mother cry.

Unfortunately, my hymen felt differently. The dozen condoms I bought sat unused on the nightstand, next to a packet of Plan B pills. Suspenders *and* a belt for me. I am a woman who buys double insurance. But my insurance proved unnecessary for my hymen refused to be obliterated, pulverized, annihilated. Its resistance to all three of Chip's attempts had not been futile. It left him whimpering and nursing himself in the dark. It sent me to Dr. Ng's examination room.

"His weenie bounced out of me like I had a trampoline down there. I must have one tough hymen. Maybe you'll need to cut it open. You can do that right?" I asked. Lying on my back on the paper-covered table, I counted the little holes in the ceiling tiles while Dr. Ng examined me with a long Q-tip.

"Actually, you're already open. I really can't see a problem," replied Dr. Ng from underneath my dressing gown.

"No, seriously, it wouldn't go in. I kept asking him what the hell was wrong with his equipment. Maybe he was too small. He was the same size as a low-absorbency tampon. Do you think that matters?"

"Uh, no, it should still work."

"That's what I thought. But anyway, I told him it wasn't his

3

fault as that's what God gave him. Then he went all floppy."

"You said that to him?"

"Yeah, I was trying to make him feel better."

"Next time, Fiona, don't try to make him feel better."

"Oh, there's not going to be a next time, Dr. Ng."

"Why is that?"

"He wouldn't let me wipe him down with an alcohol pad. You know, to sanitize that area before slipping the condom on."

"Fiona, why in the world…?"

Because he wouldn't let me boil his penis in water first.

It was all Listerine's fault—or perhaps Neosporin's. All those commercials with oversized cartoon germs in Crayola colors with spikes, tails, and little mouths eating away at the tongue and gums. All those flagella propelling fat microbes about on the skin. All those microscopic spirals, spheres, and cylinders of death and disease waiting for their chance to slip into the body. No wonder Listerine sells so well. Maybe the next guy wouldn't mind being splashed with some minty-fresh mouthwash. I'd offer him the non-stinging kind.

"You're thin, pretty, and smart. Don't worry. You'll find some-one, Fiona," said Dr. Ng, as I pulled my long hair into a French twist.

That was not the point. For nearly three decades, culture, parents, and upbringing all intertwined my self-worth with my hymen. If it was indeed that valuable, I should want to rip it out, freeze-store it in a little plastic bottle and leave an instruction in my last will and testament to be buried with it. Either that or stuff it in a little glass vial and wear it around my neck like Angelina Jolie did with Billy Bob's blood.

Anything but let someone else take it. And have a picture of me up on his MySpace page next to the other picked cherries. Or get my bloodied panties passed around in the boys' locker room.

No thank you.

Then Dr. Ng came up with the dildo solution. No rush, no fear of STDs or pregnancy, no involvement of another human being, no stench of human warmth crushing down on me. Nothing but an eternal, unfailing erection that could be twisted and bent to my satisfaction and sanitized with boiling water. God bless Dr. Ng.

But I came up with the two-percent Lidocaine gel idea. I demanded an extra-large prescription to ensure that I would have enough to cover Mr. Happy and myself several times over. With a large number of anesthetics available, I saw no reason for having to endure any pain. It wasn't as if I had asked for an epidural. That would be insane. But this? A little gel and no pain. God bless Lidocaine.

I don't think Chip would have let me slather Lidocaine all over him. But Mr. Happy remained true to his name and was more than happy to oblige.

Guys. So overrated.

I PULLED THE CAP OFF the Lidocaine bottle with my teeth, wondering if the manufacturers had anticipated how their customers were going to use their product. The bottle had a long, narrow applicator tip like a tube of Krazy Glue. The gel came out in a thin, delicate squiggle with every squeeze.

I held Mr. Happy horizontally and squirted a line of Lidocaine on him, zigzagging back and forth like I was putting spicy mustard on my Sheboygan Bratwurst at AT&T Park. I smoothed the gel out, glazing the slippery silicone surface like a Krispy Kreme.

The Internet was right. The saleslady at Good Vibrations was right. Silicone dildos are the best.

Dr. Ng had suggested that I buy a bottle of KY Jelly, originally to put on my face to treat the dryness caused by my eczema, which she noticed during my exam. Go to a dermatologist and you get Elidel cream for your face. Go to a gynecologist and you get KY Jelly.

The little two-ounce bottle with a purple cap had caused a sensation at my house. My mother refused to believe that I had bought it for my face. I couldn't blame her. After all, who goes out with a face covered in lubricant? You start your day with Clean & Clear or Noxzema. You follow it with Clinique, Origins, or Chanel, not KY.

I decided not to douse the Lidocaine-coated dildo with KY Jelly. First, I didn't want to dilute the potency of the Lidocaine. Second, KY Jelly had already caused enough trouble for me. A troublemaker. And third, I really, really didn't want to dilute the potency of the Lidocaine. Lidocaine was king.

Suddenly, it occurred to me then that what I was doing was absurd. I wondered how many women in the world went through this ritual of taking their virginity. I wondered how many prescriptions of Lidocaine had been written for this purpose. How many dildos had been used in this way.

Absurd, demented, brilliant.

After I smeared some Lidocaine inside me, I waited for the

blessed gel to take effect while I plugged in my iPod for some Nirvana. "Smells Like Teen Spirit" felt appropriate for the occasion. For me, the hallmark of any great song is its ability to endure Repeat One for hours on end without rousing me to raging violence. True for Nirvana; not true for The Doors. My college roommate had played "Light My Fire" on Repeat One for an entire evening. I had to take an Ativan to refrain myself from strangling her in her sleep with her stereo's electric cord.

I flipped off my bedroom lights.

With the lights out, it's less dangerous

How right you are, Kurt. It seemed obscene to do it under the ashy-white glow of CFL lighting. It seemed less ridiculous with the lights out. So I scooted myself on my bed and put my back against the wall. Hunched up, with my knees bent and spread apart, I must have looked like a frog, squatting on my bed and rotating Mr. Happy by the base so the Lidocaine gel would not drip off.

Twenty minutes.

Hello, hello, hello, how low?

Lower.

I pinched myself to see if I was good and numb. Excited that I could only feel my fingertips, I aimed Mr. Happy at the opening to the holy of holies.

"Go, Mr. Happy, go where no man has ever gone before." My final frontier.

"An in he throng." Just like Chaucer said. Now that man was a real poet.

I expected something, anything. A prick, a tear, a loud ripping, a shredding, a sharp puncturing like the pop of a balloon. But there was nothing like that. After a bit of initial resistance, it just felt like inserting an over-lubricated, jumbo-sized purple tampon. Parting myself like the Red Sea. Moses would be proud.

When I looked down, Mr. Happy had disappeared into the hallowed darkness. The flared base, the only part still visible, nestled up tight against me, ensuring easy extraction.

Seeing my success, I bit my lips, trying to suppress a squeal of delight. I had conquered myself. I wanted to carve a notch on my own headboard. I had picked my own cherry. I had been deflowered by my own hand. I would forever own myself, my honor, my all. My virginity will always be mine.

Penis envy my ass, you losers.

I pushed against Mr. Happy's base to keep him snug. After that ordeal, I wanted to make sure that my hymen was demolished good and proper and that it would stay that way. I didn't want it closing back in like ear piercings if you removed the earring too early.

"Twist and disinfect. Twice daily for six weeks."

This was less of a hassle.

I grabbed a piece of square cotton gauze quickly and readied myself to soak up my family's honor. I wanted to capture every drop like that man did in *Memoirs of a Geisha*. The collector with his glass vials of Asian virginity in his black bag. I would be my own collector. A collection of one.

I swabbed myself and caught nothing but globs of Lidocaine gel. I had really overdone it with the anesthetic. But better overdone than underdone. Half a bottle good, a whole bottle better. Orwell got it backwards.

A mulatto, an albino, a mosquito, my libido

Cobain was a genius. I wondered what he would have written

if he saw me like this, waiting eagerly with a pad of cotton gauze to collect the remnants of my hymen.

I thought about auctioning off my bloody gauze on eBay. Reserve price of $19.95. I wondered how many bids I would get.

My knees ached. I stood up, trying to keep Mr. Happy inside me while stretching my legs, back, and arms. Bad idea. Mr. Happy hit the hardwood floor of my bedroom with a dull thud and rolled under my bed, collecting lint, seed husks, and strands of black hair on his Lidocaine-glazed shaft.

Pepito, my parakeet, woke up and began beating his wings against the bars of his cage, protesting the violent disturbance of his sleep. Parakeets need ten to fifteen hours of sleep a day or else they'll croak. I felt bad.

I feel stupid and contagious

Leaving Mr. Happy to get acquainted with the dust bunnies under my bed, I jumped up and down, trying to shake every last drop of honor out of me. When the pad felt heavy and saturated with liquid, I removed it, glass vial ready and waiting.

But the cotton pad glistened only with a slick, glossy whiteness. Whiteness, a shiny whiteness that belonged to the porcelain god, to the driven snow, to Great White paper, to virgins.

"Some people are born without hymens," Dr. Ng had said. "Some break them during gymnastics, horseback riding, roundhouse kicking, cheerleading."

I have never done a split or straddled a horse. I have never tornado kicked anything. I have never had to do a flying herkie while waving some pompoms.

And yet, the whiteness confronted me. Bold, unflinching, unapologetic.

No blood.

No honor. My family had no honor.

I had been born without honor. I had been protecting, preserving, and defending an honor that had never even existed.

Hi, my name is Fiona Yu.

People call me Fi.

Here we are now, entertain us

It's so nice to meet you.

Oh, by the way, I'm missing a hymen.

CHAPTER
TWO

I T'S CALLED HYMEN restoration, or hymenoplasty.

No joke. In fact, it has gotten so popular in New York City that the price has gone from five thousand to eighteen hundred dollars in several clinics. Nose jobs are out. Hymen jobs are in.

And they're done by real surgeons, not perverted hacks in a dark back room without an autoclave.

The Internet is flooded with ads from hymen restoration surgeons. "Dr. Sean Killroy. Surgeon highly experienced in hymen surgery. San Francisco."

"Highly experienced" sounded good to me.

So I picked up the phone to make an appointment. I wanted the hymen that evolution had seen fit to deny me. I didn't have to have one for a wedding night. I didn't have to save myself from a village stoning. I just wanted some family honor that I could shred into bloody pieces and wear around my neck.

Kind of like women who find out they can't have babies. The doctor tells them their plumbing's no good and all of sudden that's the only thing they want. A crying, screeching baby. All because they can't have one. We want what we don't have, can't have. We decide that we must have it. That we can't live without it.

That was me.

"Two weeks?" I shouted into the phone.

"That's the earliest appointment I have for Dr. Killroy," replied the throaty voice.

There must be an epidemic destroying hymens in San Francisco. A surge of aft-regretted premarital sex. Either that or there was another serial rapist running around. I wouldn't know. I never watched the news; it just depressed me. There was always a rapist, pedophile, or psycho killer doing God's work.

"Okay, I'll take it."

"Wonderful, I'll put you in for the last appointment of the day. Four-thirty."

"Great. I won't need to take the entire day off work. Oh, how much is this going to cost?"

"Depends on what you want done."

"My hymen is missing. I want one put in."

"Oh, you were born without one?" she asked, her voice full of pity like I had just told her I was born horribly disfigured.

"Apparently so."

"Well, honey, that's not hymen restoration. There's nothing to restore. You'll need a hymen re-creation. That costs more."

"So how much is it?"

"That runs about twenty-five hundred dollars, more for complicated cases."

I had no idea whether I was a complicated case, but I took the appointment. Twenty-five hundred dollars is what it costs to get a shiny new hymen in San Francisco. Twenty-five hundred dollars and you are as pure as a newborn babe. Twenty-five hundred dollars for family honor. For the same price, you could get yourself the latest Chanel handbag. Guess it depends on what your priorities are.

I wanted a hymen more than a Chanel handbag, even though one would go nicely with all my pin-striped suits.

I AM A CORPORATE lawyer.

I went to law school because I didn't want to be a pediatrician or a gynecologist like all the other Chinese girls in my class. I didn't want to examine women's nether regions or catch newborns as they shot out of the birth canal. I didn't want to wipe dripping snot or deal with screaming babies.

Instead, I chose to deal with screaming senior partners.

I chose to stock up on industrial size Chapstick for all the ass-kissing I had to do when I wasn't billing hours. Many, many thousands of billable hours. The bane of the law profession. The yoke of all attorneys-at-law in the private sector.

On the first day of law school, the dean welcomed us with a motivational welcome speech. "When you leave here with your law degree, you will have a tremendous amount of power and privilege."

The dean must have had a different definition of power than my senior partner, Jack.

Jack of Toller & Benning LLP, Land of Lost Persons. Fat,

bald, foul-mouthed Jack. Six foot one. Fifty-eight years young. Strawberry nose of a drinker. Face of a bulldog. The biggest rainmaker in the corporate group.

As a young associate in the corporate and securities group at a five-hundred-plus lawyer law firm, I had the privilege of keeping my water under Jack's desk. All the associates did. We had the power to be his yes-men, his sycophants, his lackeys. In return, he gave us the honor of doing all his scutwork at the impressive billable rate of two hundred and seventy-five dollars an hour and the joy of working over eighty hours a week in thick, expensive suits and nylons.

Dean Perry, I want my money back.

"Power is when the other guy has to sit there with a shit-eating grin while you ejaculate right into his face," said Jack, pulling at his suspenders.

Nice man, Jack was.

Power is when you can just buy yourself a hymen for twenty-five hundred dollars without having to worry if you can still afford to eat dinner that week.

To pay for the new hymen, I had to glue myself in front of my computer screen in my office with the view of the city from the twenty-second floor behind me. I had to imprison myself in a tower of steel and glass.

But I kept little things to remind me that there was more to life than Jack, memoranda of understanding, and purchase and sale agreements.

Ted Bundy grinned at me from my computer desktop—that handsome, toothy, wolfish grin in black and white. A true psychopath. Charming, glib, and merciless.

"Who is that cutie? Is that your boyfriend?" asked my pretty secretary, eyeing my desktop picture with interest.

"Oh no, out of my league."

She laughed. "I'd wrap him around my little finger."

"Oh, he'd probably eat you right up."

Little finger included.

No wonder we Americans are so in love with our serial killers, the epitome of freedom and power. As a nation of fast cars, fast food, and perfect teeth, we are obsessed with the ones who possess complete freedom from fear, remorse, and conscience. America enjoys the prestige of having the longest list of these creatures and has spawned some of the finest specimens in the world.

China has a pathetically short list.

The Collectionist, the Angel of Death, the Alligator Man, the Vampire of Sacramento, the Freeway Killer, Son of Sam, the Hillside Stranglers, the Shoe-Fetish Slayer, the Killer Clown, the Werewolf of Wisteria, the Lipstick Killer, the Campus Killer, the Giggling Granny.

And then there was Gein, who won the Best Dressed award.

A slideshow of them saved my screen when I left my computer unattended.

A gallery of the sick and twisted. A spark of something outside the corporate world, outside of Jack.

These folks are not to be confused with psychotics, people who hear voices, who mistake themselves for Jesus, who eat their own shit, who wear aluminum foil hats to keep out alien brain waves, who get injected in the ass with Haloperidol at the end of the day while strapped onto a gurney.

No, these folks have jobs. They shower, brush their teeth,

have wives and children, attend Sunday services, participate in Boy Scouts, coach Little League, bring pot roast to the neighborhood picnic, bake you apple pie, volunteer to watch your little ones so you can go out on the town with the missus for a night.

Then they'll hog-tie you, rape you, sodomize you, burn you with their cigarette butts, bite off little chunks of your flesh, strangle you, inject bleach into your veins, carve you up like a fat Thanksgiving turkey, splatter you on the walls, ceilings, floors, before gouging out your eyes for a trophy and adding a piece of you to their nipple belt.

Or turn you into vegetable-face soup. A la Albert Fish. Five points for an ear. Ten points for a nose. And double points for a lower lip.

And for all their hard work, the state rewards these folks with the needle, gas chamber, electric chair, sparing them from the indignities of old age. No sitting in a pool of their own piss. Lucky bastards.

Bundy was right. All you have to do is comb your hair and wear a suit and you can be one crazy motherfucker. And get away with it.

The FBI profiles are almost always the same: White men. Age twenty-five to forty. Female serial killers account for only eight percent of all American serial killers. And they are white too.

White people get to have all the fun.

For once, I'd like to hear "The unsub is most likely female. Asian. Age twenty-five to forty."

Unlikely. Just look at Hello Kitty.

I hate Hello Kitty.

I hate her for not having a mouth or fangs like a proper kitty.

She can't eat, bite off a nipple or finger, give head, tell anyone to go and fuck his mother or lick herself. She has no eyebrows, so she can't look angry. She can't even scratch your eyes out. Just clawless, fangless, voiceless, with that placid, blank expression topped by a pink ribbon.

Poor Hello Kitty. Having to go around itchy, unlicked, unscratched. Tortured by her own filth.

Like my mother.

After nearly thirty years of marriage to my father, she still asks him for money to buy Payless shoes. And groceries, discount clothing, Maybelline makeup.

That's another reason I became a lawyer instead of a housewife. An American lawyer. I wanted to be able to pay for my Jimmy Choos myself with Visa, Mastercard, American Express. I never leave home without it. Thank you, Carl Malden.

So I could tell anyone who tried to put a damn bow behind my ear to go to hell. But it didn't work out that way. The six-figure salary, the J.D., the Eileen Fisher-Armani-Calvin Klein wardrobe didn't liberate me from the confines of tradition, culture, and family.

Because it's family. My family. And you don't turn your back on love and family. A J.D. doesn't change that. It's just a part of people culture.

So I became an American lawyer with Jack's shoe prints on my back any given day. An American lawyer who is expected to help out at her parents' Laundromat on the weekends after an eighty-hour week. An American lawyer who still lives at home.

MANY OF MY CHINESE FRIENDS' parents either worked at or owned a Laundromat or two somewhere in the city. Their offspring unanimously bitched and moaned about having to pitch in.

Not me.

I enjoyed my hours at the Laundromat. The Laundromat allowed me to be personally responsible for the destruction of at least three Chinese marriages from behind the counter.

"I'm so sorry, Mrs. Fung. Your clothes aren't ready yet. We are having a bit of trouble getting this cherry lipstick stain out of your husband's shirt."

Mrs. Fung, standing there bare-faced, sporting the au natural look. Mrs. Fung, who didn't own a tube of cherry lipstick.

"Just give me his shirts," she said, grim-faced.

Okay.

"Oh, Mrs. Wong, this fell out of the blazer pocket. Here you go."

It was a note with the message "Have a great day at work, honey" scrawled in large, loopy handwriting with a bright red lipstick kiss on it.

"Thank you, Fiona. You are such a good girl."

"Oh no, I only pretend to be."

I do try.

"Your husband brought these in yesterday. Just to let you know, Mrs. Lim, we don't like to handle lingerie. Too delicate," I said, holding up a silk La Perla teddy I had pulled from another customer's pile.

Mrs. Lim stared at the black negligee I was dangling in front of her. Her mouth pressed into a thin line. Her expression became wooden.

"Thank you for telling me."

You're welcome.

It was high time Hello Kitty got a mouth.

I didn't do this to every couple. Only to the ones I thought were on the brink of divorce already.

But I helped change that for the Lims, the Wongs, and the Fungs.

Chinese parents screamed, yelled, and threatened divorce only to return to their normal daily routines of cooking and cleaning and picking the kids up from school. Decade after decade, they clung to each other, fighting, bickering, and eating dinner together.

Empty threats made good, solid marriages.

Maybe saving your hymen for your husband to lay to waste on your wedding night helped too.

Unfortunately, I didn't have that precious gift to give.

Twenty-five hundred dollars and the skills of Dr. Sean Killroy, "highly skilled in hymen surgery," would give me the ability to keep that man. Decade after decade.

Two weeks.

One hundred seventy hours billed.

Thousands of pieces of clothes freshly laundered.

One lovers' quarrel caused by a carefully-placed empty condom wrapper in a trouser pocket.

And I found myself teasing Dr. Sean Killroy's porcupine puffer fish from the dry side of the tank in his waiting room.

CHAPTER
THREE

D R. SEAN KILLROY RAN a very lucrative business restoring women's hymens.

His porcupine puffer fish, with its glittering blue-green doe eyes, spiked body, human-like incisors, and its eerie smile all wiggling up to my tapping finger, told me so. So did his spotted moray eel that had slipped half its body through a plastic tube at the bottom of the tank. And his large yellow tang.

Any fish that looks like it's smiling at you will cost a lot to acquire and to keep. Those little teeth won't munch on flakes or pellets. They nibble on oysters, clams, shrimp, and sea urchins. Sea urchins. You need to rotate that diet every day or else it'll just go on a hunger strike. The puffer is a very picky fish. It requires its own sushi chef.

And it has a huge appetite.

So huge that you can only keep it with other big, colorful, expensive tropical fish to ensure that they won't end up as its lunch.

Dr. Killroy needed to repair a lot of hymens to keep his

puffer happy.

Chinatown doctors keep twenty-gallon tanks with ten five-for-a-dollar feeder goldfishes that swim back and forth in front of a cardboard backdrop. Those fishes are lucky if they get a filter. Otherwise, they just swim in their own muck.

Chinatown doctors don't repair or recreate hymens.

"Fiona Yu? The doctor will see you now."

The nurse gave me the once-over, pausing ever so slightly on my crotch. I could hear the cash register ring in her mind. Another twenty-five hundred dollars for the doctor. The little puffer would continue to enjoy its daily seafood buffet.

"Take your clothes off and put this on. Panties too. The doctor will be right with you," she said, handing me a blue dressing gown. "Opens at the back."

Duh.

I was there to get a new hymen. Of course, I would have to take my underwear off.

Panties. I hate that word. It sounds dirty. It makes me think of perverts, molesters, rapists, horny college boys.

"So, Ms. Yu, what can I do for you? I'm Dr. Sean…"

Dr. Killroy had been looking down into the opened file folder when he walked through the door. But then he looked up and stopped.

You can change your name. You can dye your hair. You can dress yourself up in new threads. But most people don't change their faces. And barring major plastic surgery, you can't change your face. The scalpel, even in the most gifted surgeon's hands, has its limitations.

Sean Killroy. Sean Smith. Sean Jones. Sean Anderson. Sean

Baxter. Sean Randall. Sean Dixon.

It didn't matter what Sean wanted to call himself these days. I recognized his dark wavy hair, his sharp, needle-like eyes and chiseled, elfin face. You never forget the face of your first best friend, the face of someone you half-loved, even if it has another sixteen years on it.

"Killroy my ass. You're Sean Deacon."

"Holy crap. Fi?"

"Yeah."

We stared at each other for a minute. If we were Peanuts characters, we would both have had large black holes for mouths.

I met Sean in the sixth grade at St. Sebastian's, courtesy of Jeremy, the biggest and meanest school bully.

Jeremy.

At the age of eleven, Jeremy already stood five foot eight inches tall. The school nurse said he had yet to go through his growth spurt. He had dirty blond hair slicked back with Dep gel. Big, cornflower-blue eyes. His thick body was an uneven mixture of fat and muscle. More fat than muscle. And sausage fingers and muddy nails bitten to the quick to boot. He needed a serious spraying of Arrid XX antiperspirant.

Jeremy loved to kick things and other students who were smaller than him. Girls in particular.

"I have strong legs, Sister. And they're bored."

And so Jeremy exercised his legs on his fellow students. He also served us all with an array of wedgies, pink bellies, knicker-bockers, and whatever suited his whim. His forte, however, was lunch-stomping. He would grab your lunch box, throw your sand-wich, leftover pizza, muffin, banana, the pork bun your mother had oh-so-carefully wrapped, onto the ground and stomp on it.

Jeremy called it food thumping.

One afternoon, Jeremy decided that my baloney sandwich needed a good thumping. He tore my blue Smurf lunch box out of my hand, opened it, and sent my Thermos, apple, and sandwich tumbling onto the tarred ground before tossing it aside. He must have been feeling especially spry as he attacked my sandwich with both feet, jumping up and down on the two slices of Wonder Bread and Oscar Mayer baloney.

I grabbed my lunch box and chased after my Thermos as it rolled down the sloping pavement into the bushes surrounding the rectory, leaving Jeremy to thump my sandwich to its demise.

I didn't cry. Crying only spurred Jeremy on. Everyone knew that. No matter how scared we were, we never cried. Jeremy would only hit you harder.

"Give *him* a thumping with that thing, Smurfette."

I turned around. A boy my age was peeking around the corner where he was smoking his cigarette, away from the ever-watchful eye of Sister Maria. He nodded at the lunch box in my hand.

"This thing? Jeremy's a solid bonehead. His skull will crack this thing in two. And my name's Fiona, not Smurfette."

"That's why you have to fill it with rocks first, Fi-*ona*," he said, jerking his head at the smooth round rocks that lined the flowerbed. "And no worries, I'll back you."

The boy winked at me.

"You're the same size as me."

"Two against one. I like those odds, don't you? Or do you prefer thumped sandwiches?"

I stared at him. I looked back at Jeremy who was bouncing

my apple against the convent wall with great enthusiasm.

"Yeah, right. I don't want to die."

"Everyone has to die. You're just scared."

"So? Aren't you?"

"No such thing as fear. Go on. I'll be right behind you. One thing, smile at him first. And don't say a word. Just clock him."

His piercing blue eyes bored into me. Their fierceness drew the fear out of me like poison from a wound.

I felt light. Calm. Like all the sound had been sucked out of the world around me. Like I had suddenly been placed in a vacuum.

Fearless.

I filled my lunch box with rocks and snapped the latch shut tight. I walked up to Jeremy who had gotten bored with my sandwich and had moved onto someone else's pizza.

"What are you looking at?" he growled.

I smiled brightly and clocked Jeremy in the face with my lunch box. Hard. And I kept swinging. And swinging. Even after he fell to the ground.

I called it jackass thumping.

Then I looked around, expecting to see my backup.

But he was nowhere to be seen.

I broke Jeremy's jaw in three places and landed myself on the bench outside Sister Carmen's office. The principal's office. The final destination for all troublemakers before they were expelled.

A familiar figure rounded the corner and sat down next to me. The boy who had called me Smurfette. He had snuck out of class.

"Thanks a lot, Charles Manson. Look where you got me."

"That was some wailing you gave him." He looked genuinely impressed.

"Shut up. And where were you?"

"You didn't need me. You had yourself covered."

"Yeah, now I'm going to get expelled. Who the hell are you anyway?"

"I'm Sean. And no, you're not. Just tell her how much you love Jesus."

Jesus. I love Jesus.

Jesus got me a major discount off of thirteen years of Catholic school education. Jesus also saved my ass every time I got into trouble with the nuns.

The nuns at St. Sebastian loved Jesus. I guess they all do. And if you loved Jesus too, they treated you better. You got better grades, a better seat, a better place in line, a better table in the cafeteria.

"I'm sorry, Sister Carmen. I'm sorry because I hurt Jeremy. And because I know what I did really hurt Jesus too."

The nuns ate that up. Being sorry for something you did because you thought it hurt Jesus. They told us that every time we did something bad, we were torturing Jesus like the Roman soldiers did.

But anything remotely fun seemed to hurt Jesus. Chewing gum, talking in class, passing notes, forgetting to do your homework, smoking, food thumping.

Problem is that God seemed to have made poor Jesus specifically for suffering. First the Cross and then the daily antics of millions of school children.

Sister Maria said God made us in His image. Me, Sean, Jeremy, all of us.

God must be a sadist. He made us all to hurt Jesus like He did. And He made it fun too. Poor Jesus.

Sean was right though.

I didn't get expelled. Instead, Jeremy did because he wasn't sorry for hurting Jesus like I was. Him and his broken jaw.

After that, Sean and I became best friends.

BUT ONE DAY, FATE took Sean away. Stephanie told the whole class Sean was gay because he wouldn't kiss her. So he lit her hair-sprayed head on fire with his Zippo lighter.

Poor Sean.

Not even Jesus and all His angels could save him.

I heard that he set someone else on fire after he got expelled.

Maybe that was why he changed his name, to erase his naughty schoolboy past. And probably because no one wanted a hymen surgeon who had a history of setting people on fire.

"I changed my name."

"Yeah, I can see that. And became a hymen restoration surgeon. How did you settle on that?"

"Atonement for all the ones I had demolished in my disrespectful youth. That and the money's great. Hey, you mind if I smoke? I can open that window there."

"God, Sean, yes. Asthma, remember? Besides, I thought doctors knew better."

"Lies. All lies about smoking. It's good for your health. Warms your lungs good and proper."

"With tar and nicotine." I laughed. Sean. Still funny after all those years.

"Everyone has to die. So what brings you in?"

"Sean, I'm missing a hymen."

"How do you know?"

"I tried to take my own virginity with a dildo covered in two-percent Lidocaine."

Sean just stared at me.

"I see. And?"

"And nothing. I was all ready to soak up my blood with some gauze and nothing."

"Fi, why?"

"So I could keep it for myself."

"Like that creepy guy in the geisha movie?"

"Something like that. And it was really interfering with my dating life. Dad wants me to find a man and get married."

"Wait, Fi. I'm twenty-eight. That means you're twenty-eight. And you've never…?"

"Sean, I'm Chinese. It's complicated. And no, it's not like I've been living in an Afghan cave. I just never went all the way. Besides, you know anyone who wants to marry me by the third date?"

"Fi, why would *you* want to marry anyone by the third date? You never know. The guy could be a complete psycho."

Sean had a good point. He would know.

"Actually, I don't want to get married. Hell, I don't even want to date."

"What?"

"Hate dealing with another person's crap. Takes time away from me. Told you. Dad's idea."

"Then why bother?"

"Humor me. Chinese mental gymnastics. Just go with it."

"Fi, who cares if you have a hymen or not?"

"I do."

"Do you need one? I mean, is your dad marrying you off to a Chinese boy that won't have you unless you have one? I assume your dad is not going to have you lynched by a mob."

"No. Just feel like I should have one like every other girl. Why? You think it's a bad idea?"

"Sort of, but let me get this straight. You want me to create you a hymen so that you can pop it with a dildo yourself? So that you can go out and date even though you don't want to?"

"Kinda. I feel robbed of the experience by cruel Mother Nature. Yeah, is that too weird?"

Sean laughed. "A little, but you know that rupturing a hymen is quite painful, right? As I recall, you used to be… how do I put it? Highly pain-averse."

"Used to be."

"Fi, you drowned that dildo in Lidocaine. You probably used the whole damn bottle."

Another good point. Sean had a knack for making lots of them.

I smiled sheepishly and snorted. I had used the whole damn bottle. "I was going to ask for another prescription for some more."

Sean rolled his eyes.

"God, Fi, save your twenty-five hundred dollars. Forget the hymen. Get yourself a Chanel handbag to go with that suit. Be happy you weren't born with a hymen, got spared the pain, and have some good sex."

Sean was right. Again.

"Doctor's orders?"

"Yeah. And one more thing. What are you doing on Saturday?"

"Depends."

"On what?"

"On why you are asking."

"I was wondering if you wanted to hang out. So we could catch up on…oh, what is it? The last sixteen years?"

"Sure, Sean. I'd love to."

"Great. And you can fill me in on whatever happened to that bitch, Stephanie."

CHAPTER
FOUR

THE CANTONESE WORD for "yes" is "hai," if you pitch your voice down.

The Cantonese word for "cunt" is "*hai*," if you pitch your voice up.

Anyone who claims that Mandarin is a better language than Cantonese needs to develop an appreciation for the fine subtlety of pitch, inflection, and intonation that can make "yes" sound like "cunt."

I love Cantonese. I can express myself at a whole new level of crudeness and vulgarity that I can't with English. That and it comes in handy when I have to deal with my parents.

Until I was twenty-three, my father always said, "Stay in school and don't get pregnant, Fi."

Hai, Daddy.

The morning after the day I learned that I had passed the California Bar Exam, my father came into my room and issued a new directive for the new chapter in my life.

"Now that you've passed the bar, it's time for you to find yourself a darling and settle down."

Hai, Daddy.

That was my father's way of saying, "Fi, you need to move out of my house."

But at twenty-three, I saw no reason to move out. It wasn't as if I was mooching off my parents. I paid rent. I paid for food. Yes, I got laundry done for free. But I insisted on doing the laundry myself. After all, I enjoyed conversing with the laundromat customers.

For the next five years, I tried to heed my father's new decree, but the hymen I never had kept getting in the way. That and a couple of other things.

At twenty-eight, my father concluded that I had failed miserably at the task of landing a husband. So he decided that he needed to take a more proactive approach to ensure my happiness, my domestic bliss.

"You are almost thirty. You need to get married."

But the damage had been done, thanks to my maternal grandmother. When I was nine years old, my family and I visited her in Hong Kong. She feared for my future in America. Land of loose morals. She thought that if I started dating, I would lose focus on my education, become a teenage unwed mother, and condemn my family to shame. So she had to save me.

"Boys will ruin your life," my grandmother said. "Boys are dirty."

To drive her point home, she unbuttoned her blouse to reveal a pair of breasts that had nursed seven children. Think Ms. Chokesondick from *South Park*. The flopping, elongated boobs swung like dual pendulums past her naval, marking the passage of time and multiple pregnancies.

"You want boyfriend? This is boyfriend," she said, shaking her baby-ruined tits at me violently. "You want to be fat? You want to look like this? You go touch boys."

If my grandmother's display wasn't enough, Eddie Martin's present certainly put me off dating. Eddie developed a crush on me in the fourth grade. Unlike other boys who gave gumball machine jewelry to the objects of their affection, he gave me a pair of ears. Two little pink discs of flesh that had previously belonged to Sammie, the science class hamster.

I couldn't wear them. They didn't have any earring posts. All they did was stink up my desk.

So when my father started pestering me about marriage, I threw myself on my bed with Pepito squatting on my left index finger. Pepito. Forty grams of pure love. Pepito with his yellow feathers and dark squiggly lines, whom I had named after the iconic boy in the yellow shirt who rode around on his bicycle yelling "chicle, chicle" in every movie filmed in Mexico.

God must have a thing for birds. He gave them convex, paunchy bellies. If He had given them concave bellies, no one would put up with their seed-throwing, screaming, nipping, and constant pooping. Most-used anuses in the world.

"I already found the love of my life, Daddy. See?" I said, planting a large kiss on Pepito's head.

Pepito squawked and nipped me on the upper lip. Hard.

"Stop kissing that thing. It's dirty."

"No, he's not. He's yummy." I licked Pepito's head.

Pepito blinked, fluffed up his feather, and scratched himself

33

with his foot. He sneezed in my face. I kissed him on his ceres.

"Fiona, stop that. You'll get SARS."

Hai, Daddy.

SARS come from infected Chinese chickens. Pepito is an American hand-fed parakeet. Born and raised in San Francisco. Pepito does not have SARS.

"You're twenty-eight. All of your cousins are already married."

All of my cousins are morons. They went to community college and pushed dim sum carts around for a living. One of them worked as a cashier at Radio Shack. They didn't walk around with twenty-five hundred dollar handbags.

"You need to find a husband."

Like I need brain cancer.

Pepito bore down on my finger and laid a solid dropping. Dark green, perfectly round, topped with a dollop of white goo. My mother called them Pepito's doughnuts.

"See, Daddy. Pepito and I are engaged. He gave me a ring." I wiggled my fourth finger, graced with Pepito's fresh doughnut. Pepito hopped onto my shoulder.

"Fi, that's disgusting. Go wash your hands. Stop acting like you are five years old. You are a lawyer. You are twenty-eight. Your mother and I have decided to help you find a husband."

Pepito regurgitated some half-digested seeds and tried to push them into my mouth. That was his way of saying "I love you."

I spat them out.

"No, I don't want a husband. I like my life with you, Mom, and Pepito just fine."

I was happy being single. I was good at being single. And God loved me way too much to inflict on me a provincial life of diapers, dining sets, and Disneyland vacations. Because I loved Jesus so much.

Not like Laurie.

Laurie Wong worked in the office next to mine in the corporate group. Same age. Chinese-American. Five foot seven. A little on the chunky side. Face like a pie. And desperate for a Chinese husband. He had to be Chinese.

When Laurie wasn't busy billing, she was man-hunting. Asian bars, Asian professional events, Asian movie night at the Kabuki Theater, Asian Art Museum, Asian moon cake eating contest in Chinatown, Asian speed-dating, Asian dating websites, Asian matchmaking, blind dates. You name it, Laurie did it.

Too bad Chinese boys didn't like her. Too fat. Too unpretty. Too successful. Too powerful. Too demanding. Too educated. Too Chinese.

"I don't feel like I need to dress up that much for a date. I want someone to like me for me," Laurie said, with her unshaven legs and raggedy ponytail.

Eddie Bauer and Hush Puppies. Her date outfit.

Too all-American.

Her only hope was to be a green card ticket.

But I didn't want to be anyone's green card ticket, meal ticket, cook, washing lady, housemaid, personal masseuse, baby machine, regularly-scheduled-hole in the mattress. Only to end up dead, discarded, buried in a ditch somewhere, dumped into the big, blue sea, all used up.

Boys should just stay home and fuck their mothers.

Maybe I should thank my missing hymen for saving me from serious relationships. And along with them a boat load of grief,

35

man troubles, and probable death.

"YOU NEED A NICE Chinese boy," my father said.

With a chicken thermometer for a penis and an ego the size of Texas.

No thank you.

"I've been asking around Chinatown. My friend has a son who…"

"Dad, you just want me to end up a headless skeleton with barnacles, washing up on shore. Your unborn grandson as fish food," I wailed loudly.

"I didn't tell you to go and marry a black man!"

White. Scott Peterson is white, Dad.

"Or end up with my head cut off, connected to my body by a thin sinew. My throat slashed. Slumped in a driveway."

"That's why I keep telling you not to date white men. They have bad tempers."

Black. O.J. Simpson is black, Dad.

"So it's better to float face down in the backyard pool in Cupertino like Jason Cai's wife?"

Poor woman had to die in Cupertino.

Like Sean said, "Everyone has to die." But the last place on earth I wanted to die was in a town like Cupertino. Asian suburbia. I would feel like such a failure, a nobody, a nameless yellow face fading into nothingness.

My father said nothing. He shuffled off.

Thank you, Jason Cai. The Asian community tried to make it the Chinese Laci Peterson case. The world disagreed. A Chinese immigrant who was not pregnant just didn't hold the same appeal. No one was interested in a dead green card whore.

The papers claimed that Jason had fallen in love with his wife Silicon Valley style. Over email. He married his wife who was fourteen years his junior and brought her to the States from Shanghai to live the American dream.

Six weeks after their wedding, her eighty-seven pound body was found floating in their pool behind their suburban home in Cupertino.

Welcome to America.

Jason's lawyer got him off. A few years later, he killed someone else. He must have been desperate to land himself in jail. Just like O.J.

A little while later, my father walked into my room again.

"You have a date this Saturday. Wear lipstick."

"What? What do you mean I have a date?"

"I have already set it up."

"I can't, Dad. I have plans this Saturday. I'm hanging out with an old friend."

"A man?"

"Yes, I do believe he is a man. But I'll double-check with him when I see him. I'm sure he wouldn't mind."

"Talk like a lady, Fi. Bad girl."

My father left the room and returned a moment later.

"Okay, you have a date this Sunday. Wear lipstick."

I tried to object, but Pepito was shoving something into my mouth. I spat it out. It was one of his doughnuts. That was his way of saying "fuck you" for spitting out his well-intentioned vomit.

Hai.

CHAPTER
FIVE

O N SATURDAY, SEAN'S CALL woke me up at around eight-thirty in the morning. I had expected to have brunch, lunch, or dinner with him, but not breakfast.

"Hey Fi, you up?"

"Well, now I am," I replied groggily.

"Good. I'm swinging by in half an hour to pick you up."

"What? What time is it? And where are we going?"

"It's time to get up. No need to put on makeup for me. Dress warm. We'll be outdoors." Sean hung up.

I rolled out of bed, brushed my teeth, and threw on a t-shirt, sweatshirt, jeans, and tennis shoes. Just as I was about to sip my hot morning tea, my cell phone rang again.

"I'm outside, Fi."

Sean waved at me inside his shiny, black Mercedes. I got in the front passenger seat, yawned, and leaned my head back on the headrest.

"God, Sean. I wasn't expecting you until a little later."

"Carpe diem. Didn't you watch that movie?"

"Well, I can't carpe the diem until I have some breakfast in me. Can we stop off to get something to eat?"

Sean tossed a Noah's Bagels bag at me and handed me a cup of coffee. "Here. Thought you would say that."

An asiago bagel with sun-dried tomato smear. Still warm from the toaster oven. For the early hour, it was better than a five-course meal at Gary Danko.

"I might need that hymen after all, Sean," I mumbled with my mouth full of bagel as Sean drove.

"Really?"

"My father is sending me on a date tomorrow night with the son of one of his Chinatown friends."

"Ooh, who's Prince Charming?"

"How the hell should I know? 'You have a date on Sunday. Wear lipstick.' That's all he said."

Sean laughed and nearly sprayed coffee on the steering wheel.

"You should show up wearing *only* lipstick. You'll bag that boy in no time. I'll be going to your wedding next Saturday."

"Shut up. It's not funny. That guy will probably bring his grandmother, mother, father, and the whole family."

"Of course, they need to check out and approve his future bride. Pinch your ass. See if you are good child-bearing material."

"No kidding. Every time my father sets me up, it's always some fat Chinese guy who can't speak English and needs to get a lifetime supply of Proactiv. Who is more interested in reaching level thirteen on World of Warcraft than…"

"Dating you?"

"Yes, Sean. Yes."

"So don't go. Tell your dad you're dating me." Sean winked.

"Yeah, right. First, he doesn't like white guys. Second, he still remembers that little incident with you setting Stephanie's head on fire. I don't think he'll be too thrilled about me hanging out with you."

"So tell him not to date white guys. You didn't tell him about today then?"

"God no. Told him I had to go into the office. What am I? Stupid?"

"Never. You're highly cerebral and darkly twisted. My dream girl. Speaking of Stephanie, whatever happened to her after I turned her into a candle?"

It was sick, but I couldn't help but laugh. I almost choked.

"Well, your little stunt burnt half her face, Sean. I heard she got pretty disfiguring scars from it. Her parents took her out of St. Sebastian's. The word was that she attended high school for a year, but the kids made fun of her too much. I think she was home schooled for a while. Then she hung herself from the shower rod when she was sixteen."

"Bitch had it coming."

"Sean, she wasn't that bad."

"What? Do you have amnesia? As I recall, you had a photographic memory."

"I still do."

"She told everyone I was a fag because I wouldn't kiss her. When my dad got wind of that, he beat the crap out of me for a week straight. He swore to beat the faggot out of me. Useless, as I didn't have any in me."

"Oh, right. I remember that."

Stephanie had been the prettiest girl in our class. And it naturally followed that she had also been the meanest girl as well. She had believed that any guy she wanted was automatically hers.

Sean had felt differently, thanks to his mother. Beautiful, flirtatious, and inappropriately oversexed, Sean's mother's blatant sexuality embarrassed him at every PTA meeting. One time, Sean and I had volunteered to distribute name tags at the welcoming table. A striking, heavily made-up brunette in tight red jeans and a see-through Spandex top sauntered up to us. She wasn't wearing a padded bra.

"So which one is your teacher, baby?" she asked Sean.

"Here you go, Mom," he mumbled as he handed her the name tag.

"Tell me it's that cutie there."

"No, Mom, that's Father O'Malley. He's the parish priest."

"How lovely. A man of the cloth. See you later, baby." She walked off towards Father O'Malley, swaying her hips.

As heads turned to follow her undulating hourglass figure, Sean averted his face and cursed.

It was the first time I had heard anyone say "fuck."

And it was then I suspected why Sean didn't seem to care for the prettiest girls at St. Sebastian's. They reminded him of his mother. Like Stephanie.

But Sean hated bullies more than he hated flirty women, thanks to his dad who was a mean son of a bitch. Sean's father never came to PTA meetings. He just sent Sean to school with bruises on his back and belly. Sean showed me behind the rectory. Back then, child abuse was not as hot a media topic as it is now. Back then, Catholic priests were enjoying fun times with altar boys with impunity.

"So how are your parents, Sean?" We had driven over to Lake Merritt in Oakland. Sean was circling around for a parking spot.

"They're dead. The old man finally drank himself to death about seven years ago. And my mother followed him a year after that. Breast cancer. She had a lump the size of a cherry tomato, but refused to see a doctor. Thought that ignoring it would make it go away. It made *her* go away in the end."

"Oh, Sean. I'm so sorry."

"She was just afraid to lose her tits. So she lost her life instead. Stupid. Here, you want some of this onion bagel? Taste it and tell me how good it is." He handed me another bagel.

"What do you mean? Can't you taste it yourself?"

"Nope, all tastes like cardboard to me. Some fat kid named Darrell, who raped his sister, shoved a pencil up my nose at juvie. Lost my sense of smell permanently."

"Oh my God. I'm afraid to ask what happened to him."

Sean looked up at me with a mischievous grin.

"You're eating. I'll tell you later." He winked at me again.

I laughed. "Poor kid. Whatever you did to him, Sean, Darrell had it coming."

"Yes. Yes, he did."

"SO WHAT HAPPENED TO you after St. Sebastian's?" I asked him after we parked.

Sean began pulling out a shotgun. Clay pigeon shooting over

43

Lake Merritt. This early in the morning, I should have guessed. Sean had been an excellent marksman with his slingshot when he was a kid. He took out a rat's eye once at his house with a single shot.

"Well, juvie for one. Lucky for me Stephanie didn't die, so they let me out when I turned eighteen. Changed my name. Fast tracked college and medical school in Puerto Rico. Surgery residency. Blah, blah. Here I am."

"Holy crap. I am in the presence of greatness."

"Thank you, thank you. And you became a liayer?" Sean smiled as we walked toward the lake.

"Please. No lawyer jokes. I've heard them all. But yes, college, law school, then husband hunting."

"Well, your father will have that covered for you. No worries."

"God. I've been trying to tell him for ages that I don't date Asian guys."

"Why not? Penises too small? It's not like you're a sex maniac. Hell, I doubt you even have a libido."

"What? Why would you say that?"

"If you had a raging libido, your first time wouldn't have been with a dildo dipped in Lidocaine at the fine age of twenty-eight. You would be out dressed like a slut in some bar, trying to catch yourself a man. Any man. If you were a lesbian, you'd be doing the same thing, but in a lesbian bar. But instead, you are spending the day with yours truly, bitching about your arranged date tomorrow night."

Sean hit the nail on the head. He had a special talent for that sort of thing.

IN THE SEVENTH GRADE, Sean and I decided to dress up as Sisters of Perpetual Indulgence for Halloween. That year, the Sisters had angered the Catholic Church with some raucous public paddling. The Church got mad because the Sisters had been enjoying it.

The nuns at St. Sebastian's denounced the Sisters as hand-maidens of the Devil himself. Abominations against God. They were here with the sole purpose of hurting Jesus.

So Sean got us two nun outfits and some cheap makeup from Walgreens. He took one look at me and said, "Christ, Fi. You look like a real nun. Sister Maria's going to love you."

Of course, he was right.

When Sister Maria saw me, she said, "How adorable! Fiona wants to be a nun. Isn't she sweet? You've made Jesus very happy. But not that much eyeshadow, dear."

I didn't realize then that I was Hello Kitty in a habit. Being yellow and having a vagina meant I couldn't pull off the Sister of Perpetual Indulgence outfit. Being Hello Kitty sucked.

When Sister Maria saw Sean, she called his mother and sent him home.

White boys had all the fun.

AND SEAN WAS RIGHT again now.

Even though I never told Sean about Grandmother or Eddie

45

Martin. Or about Uncle Yuen.

When I was seven, my parents dragged me on a fourteen hour flight back to China to visit some of my cousins. At their house, boys were allowed first dibs on all dishes at mealtimes. Girls had to wait until they took all the chicken drumsticks, wings, all the good parts. So of course, I grabbed my fork (because my Chinese cousins assumed I didn't know how to use chopsticks, being American and all) and nabbed a prime piece of chicken in protest.

I got sent out to the open yard for my audacity even though it was raining. That's what happens when Hello Kitty refuses to play according to the rules. She gets sent out in the rain. Blackballed, ostracized, shunned, punished.

Uncle Yuen paid me a visit out there. He was what people called a funny uncle. Not because he was full of laughs, but because he tried to tickle me in all the bad places. Alone, out in the rain, vulnerable. Hello Kitty was a sitting target until a flock of roosting pigeons suddenly took off from the roof and distracted him.

I had left the lunch table so suddenly that I didn't realize I had taken my fork with me. I stabbed his hand with it. His tickling days were over.

That's why I love birds. I really owed them one.

"I THINK YOU MIGHT BE onto something, Sean. I don't like touching people. The feel of another's bone and flesh reminds me too much of my own mortality. Creepy." And of my funny uncle in China.

"Yeah, that might be an issue with dating someone, Fi."

"No shit. I'm a loner. Doomed forever to wander the moors alone."

"Not necessarily. You could marry this Asian boy."

"I told you, Sean. I don't date Asian guys."

"Oh yeah, why?"

"Two reasons. One called Theo. The other, Keith." I kept the other reasons to myself.

Sean waved to a man in a thick blue jacket, who looked up as we walked over. He had been loading the traps with clay pigeons. Seeing us, he straightened up and held out his hand. "Nice to see you again, Sean."

Sean shook his hand. "Max, this is my friend, Fiona. We're going to do a little shooting today. Over there."

"Nice to meet you, Fiona. Okay. Let me know when you guys are ready."

We wandered a little ways further and stopped as Sean loaded his shotgun. "PULL!" He bellowed.

A clay pigeon shot into the air.

Sean aimed and fired. Crack.

The orange target shattered.

"Nice, Sean."

"Thank you. So, what are you waiting for, Fi? Dish. I know you're dying to. Theo. Keith."

Even when we were in the sixth grade, I always had the sneaking suspicion that Sean could read minds. Although his uncanny ability had impressed me, it had also frightened me. It was like having Counselor Deanna Troi for a best friend.

"Theo. High school boyfriend for a week. Korean guy."

"Boyfriend for a week? Wow, a long, serious relationship, I

see. Your dad must have been thrilled."

"My dad didn't know. Anyway, Theo's parents were both doctors. Well-educated. Wealthy, but country bumpkins at heart. Lived up in a four-story house near where Robin Williams used to live in the Pacific Heights. His father regularly beat his mother to a pulp, causing the neighbors to call the police. He thought wife-beating was his birthright because he had a yellow penis."

"I hope you convinced him otherwise."

"Nah, left that to some other lucky woman. Hence, a week."

"I see, and Keith?"

"Oh no. I'm not done with Theo. He also had this thing where his little toe kept falling off."

Sean snorted. "PULL!"

Crack.

"His little toe kept falling off?"

"That's what he told me. Said he had to keep going to the hospital to get it re-attached."

"Did you ever see this, Fi?"

"No, why would I want to?"

"Then please tell me you didn't buy his bullcrap."

"Nah, I'd figured that he was fibbing. Sounded too incredible."

"Yeah, I'll say."

"He also had a mentally ill grandmother who regularly ate her own shit."

Sean lowered his shotgun and stared at me.

"Did you just say that she ate her own shit?"

"Yup, and not only that, she believed that her fecal matter was so nutritious she slipped some into the family dinner when they weren't looking. They had to lock her in her room while

48

they cooked. Not joking."

Sean stared at me with wide eyes. I noticed how very beautiful they were.

"Christ, Fi. Tell me you never ate dinner at his house."

"What are you, crazy? Meatloaf with a taste of grandma for dinner and watch his dad beat his mother for entertainment afterwards? No thank you."

"When you put it that way, makes me think you missed out on some serious family entertainment at his house."

"God, thanks to Theo, I didn't date another Asian guy until Keith last year."

"Ah, Keith. Please tell me he didn't eat his own shit."

"No, worse. He ate his cats' crap."

"Fi, you've got to be kidding me. You are one weirdo magnet. Where did you meet this guy?"

"Tell me about it. Keith. Chinese. Met him in salsa class. By the way, worst music in the world. Does nothing but give me migraines."

"Me too. I'd rather bang my head on some cymbals. But wait, your dad let you go salsa dancing?"

"Of course, guys all around."

"Got it. Go on."

"Keith fancied himself an architect. Ninety-nine percent ego, one percent questionable talent."

Sean laughed. "Harsh, aren't you?"

"But true. Thought he was the next Le Corbusier. My ass. Everything Keith designed looked like a matchbox that would roast people in the summer and freeze them in the winter. But what he lacked in talent and ability, he made up for in ego."

"That's it? You know, Fi, score on the loser scale is usually inversely proportional to penis size."

I threw my head back and laughed loudly. God bless Sean.

"You might be right. Keith was a major loser. He believed he was special because he thought of himself as a hippie. Because he was not 'mainstream.' What a retard."

"Awww, gross, Fi. I hate hippies. Nothing special about surviving on rabbit food and not showering. Doesn't make you special, just stupid and disgusting."

"Oh my God, no shit. He had to eat all organic food. We're not just talking tomatoes here. From bread to cookies to rice to the onions he put into his stir fry. And you know what I noticed? If organic food is so damn good for you, why did all the people who shop at those organic markets look so bad? They all looked wrinkled and dirty. My God, the chemicals must be doing something good for us."

"Hippies. What did you expect? Well, at least he cooked."

"I wished he didn't. He was such a loser. He got fired from a proper architectural firm because he couldn't play well enough with others. So he decided to start his own firm in the back room of his apartment. He didn't make enough money to feed himself properly because he insisted on eating organic everything. So he starved half the time and wanted me to do the same. That and every time he made dinner, we both got diarrhea. And I finally found out why. He was a big believer in composting…"

"PULL!"

Crack.

I watched as the shattered pieces fell into the lake.

"Oh no, I'm not sure that I want to hear the rest of this story."

"Too bad. I've already started. Composting. Good idea in theory, not in practice. It just stinks and you have to be really careful or you'll just contaminate your food and poison yourself. Well, you'll never believe where he kept his compost heap."

"Where?"

"In the bottom shelf of his fridge, next to uncovered food."

"Aw, Gawd. Disgusting. No wonder you guys had the shits. How long were you with this loser?"

"I'm so embarrassed. Four months, four months too long."

"Four months and you didn't sleep with him?"

"Nope."

"See? No libido."

"Whatever. I wasted enough life on him."

"Why? Because you liked him or because you were hoping to land a husband to please your dad?"

"Honestly, I have no idea. I wanted to shove cat shit into his mouth every time he said 'organic.'"

"What did your dad think of Keith?"

"Nothing. I didn't tell him anything."

"Let me guess, lots of all-nighters at the office?"

I laughed. Sean was sharp as ever.

"So you said Frank Gehry wannabe ate cat shit?"

"He did. He had two cats, but never cleaned his apartment. So there was hair everywhere all the time. Like an inch thick. And he put both litter boxes next to the fridge. The dinner table was in the kitchen. So in the middle of dinner, our food would sometimes smell like cat shit when the cats came in to do their business."

"Oh God. You know. If you smell it, you're eating it. So you were both eating cat shit."

"Thank you, Sean. That helps so much."

"You're welcome. So two shit-eating weirdos and no more Asian guys for you, huh?"

"Christ. How many, then? Two was two too much."

"They can't all be that *interesting*."

"Well, I guess I'm about to find out, aren't I? Daddy has several of them all lined up for me, I imagine. Sunday is only the beginning. You just wait and see."

"Oh, I will." He grinned.

When Sean dropped me off at my house, I suddenly remembered something.

"Hey, Sean. So what ever happened to Darrell?"

"Oh, he had a little accident."

"Sean."

"Fi."

"Sean, what did you do?"

"Nothing. He was smoking in bed, which of course is a big no-no. He fell asleep and set himself on fire."

I stared at Sean.

"What? He did, Fi."

"Uh-huh. Did he survive?"

"No, regrettably, Darrell the rapist did not make it."

"Why am I not surprised, Sean?"

Sean stared straight ahead with his hands on the steering wheel. He smiled out into the view in front of him.

"Because you know me too well."

CHAPTER
SIX

MAYBE IT WOULDN'T have been so bad to be a nun. Three meals a day, decent housing, uniform wardrobe, no need to keep up with ever-changing fashion. No need to outshine the other nuns with a snazzier habit. You could even hide a bad haircut or a nasty hair day under the veil. Imagine all the money a girl could save on makeup, hair products, jewelry, and shoes.

And the only thing you had to do was to pretend to love Jesus all the time and deal with bratty children every day.

In exchange, no man would ever expect you to put out no matter how many times you smiled at him. After all, you'd be married to Jesus. Only an idiot would dare to piss off Jesus.

And no man would ever expect to see you in four-inch pointy-toed stilettos on a date.

Ever.

Women bitch to other women abut how much their feet are killing them because misery loves company. Women bitch to men about how much their feet are killing them to get a foot rub or to initiate foreplay.

Not me.

If stilettos didn't hurt so much, I would never wear them. I actually like what the pain represents. The physicality of life. The feeling that an actual soul inhabits this shell of flesh and bone.

When you are in good health, you don't feel your body. You walk around inside it, but you don't feel it. It's only when something is wrong that you feel anything. I can't blame the folks who like to cut themselves. Probably jolts them out of numbness.

But I don't like razor blades. Too sharp. Too painful. Too disfiguring. Too ghetto. Too big a risk of infection—even though you can boil them in water to sanitize them. And all those cartoon germs, waiting and ready to slither in through the cut and devour the body from inside out. It's not like I can inject myself with Listerine.

I'm also too vain to blemish my milky white skin.

Milky white skin, the hallmark of Asian beauty. You can be as fat as Dom DeLuise. You can even look like Dom DeLuise and sprout some facial hair. If you have white skin, you're considered beautiful.

Just ask my cousin Katie.

Katie lived in Los Angeles. I visited her for Christmas one time.

"You're too dark and too fat," Katie told me. We were still at the terminal at LAX.

Me at one hundred five pounds. Five foot three inches. Shade NC25 in MAC Cosmetics. Too dark and too fat.

Katie at ninety pounds. Five foot five inches. Shade C15 in

MAC Cosmetics. She bleached her skin. Her skin was so white it had a tinge of lavender to it. She also fainted all the time.

It costs four hundred and fifty dollars for half an ounce of Japanese skin lightener. And that's the low-end stuff. The really good stuff with pure mulberry extract will set you back at least eight hundred and fifty dollars. Whiteness doesn't come cheap.

Katie's face resembled a pork bun the size of a stop sign. Big, round, doughy, flat.

My face is more angled. I have a more distinct jawline. My eyes are larger.

But Katie was considered more beautiful. Because she bleached her skin with eight hundred and fifty dollar skin lightener.

I don't bleach my skin.

I don't cut myself with razor blades.

Instead, I wear painful, pointy four-inch stilettos day in and day out. The perfect combination of beauty and pain. Stilettos accentuate my legs, hips, torso. They give me height to hold my too-dark-unbleached face up to the world. My constant foot pain reminds me that I am indeed alive inside my body.

And because it's a lot more sanitary than cutting.

The pain is really quite exquisite.

I love the way my toes jam into the narrow toebox, the excruciating crunch they suffer for the price of fashion and beauty. I love how my arches flex up almost beyond their capability. I love how pain shoots up my ankles, calves, knees, and thighs with every pounding step I take on the pavement, grounding me in my physical body.

I also like that it's my secret pain. Crammed in Jimmy Choo, Prada, Dior, Louboutin, Sergio Rossi, Versace, Manolo Blahnik,

Via Spiga. Private, delicious, designer hell connecting me to this earthly plane.

So I wear stilettos. Even when I'm not on a date.

It's the modern version of Chinese footbinding.

Bound feet captivated Chinese men for almost a thousand years despite the awful smell it produced. I wonder if I walked around the Financial District screaming, "God, my feet are killing me! My feet are killing me!" what would happen. Maybe some handsome man would throw himself at me. Then maybe my father wouldn't have to set me up on dates with Chinese boys like Freddie.

FREDDIE.

On Sunday evening, I slipped into a silk, maroon halter dress and a pair of four-inch Roberto Cavalli stilettos. I knew that I was overdressed for a man like Freddie. I just wanted to flaunt what he could never have in his face.

"So can you cook?" Freddie asked.

Freddie. Five foot seven inches. Twenty pounds overweight. Pock-marked. Skin darker than a donkey's ass. Broken English. Napoleon Dynamite glasses. No joke. My father could really pick them.

"So what do you do, Freddie?"

"I like to play video games."

"No, what do you do? For a living."

"I work in a computer store."

"Like Comp USA?"

"No, smaller."

Freddie continued to stuff pan-fried noodles into his pock-marked face. My father had set us up in his favorite hole-in-the-wall Chinatown café. Perhaps he didn't think Freddie could afford to take me anywhere else.

Freddie looked up.

"Why aren't you eating?" he asked with a mouthful of noodles. One fell, slipped out of his mouth and back onto his plate.

"Oh. No appetite." One look. I was already full.

"So do you cook?" Freddie asked for a second time.

"Do I look like I can cook?"

"I need a woman who can cook. Like my mom."

I need a man who I can tuck away in a drawer. Like my Mr. Happy.

"Do you do laundry? My mom says you can do laundry."

"No. I soil laundry."

"Because I need someone who can do laundry."

Of course a man like Freddie needed someone to cook and to do laundry. He wasn't going to get to level thirteen on Final Fantasy IV all by himself.

"So what do you like to do, man?"

Freddie winced. "You don't talk like a lady."

Asshole.

"Let me guess, dude. Video games. Mahjong. Jade Channel melodrama."

Jade Channel 360 on Comcast. The Chinese cable channel that shows Hong Kong mini-series about ungrateful sons, struggling mothers, and unrequited love. My parents live on Jade

57

Channel shows.

"Why, yes. What's wrong with that?"

"Oh, nothing, Freddie. So do you have any pets?"

"What?"

"Pets. Little animals you keep for fun."

"Oh, I have a pet turtle."

"The little quarter-sized ones from Chinatown fairs?"

"Yup. Aren't you going to eat some more? Fiona, right?"

"Yeah, dude. I'm working on it. So what's your turtle's name?"

"Fei. Because it sounds like my name, Freddie. You have a pet?"

"Yes, I have a parakeet, Pepito." Because it didn't sound anything like my name.

"Oh, I hate birds. Noisy and dirty things."

I just stared. Stared at the bird-hating lump of a man.

You go to hell, man. You go to hell and you die. Pepito is twice the boy you are. Pepito has a foot fetish. He'll shrimp my toes, nibble on them, shit on them. He'll give me ample foot pain in beak-sized bites, you motherfucker. Go home and eat your mother's goddamn wonton soup. And drop dead.

Freddie pushed his chair back and got up.

"I have to go to the bathroom. And step out back for a smoke."

A smoker to boot. How lovely.

Freddie walked towards the back of the restaurant.

Twenty minutes.

Still no Freddie. All he left behind was an empty, oily plate and the check. The bastard probably snuck out the back way.

I threw down a twenty-dollar bill and left the restaurant. Outside, a light rain had started to fall. I wrapped my long, wool coat tighter around me and wished that I had checked the weather before I left the house.

A horn honked, and I turned around. I saw Sean waving at me from inside his car. God bless Sean. Perfect timing. Sean always seemed to have perfect timing. Just like the day we met. Just in time to rescue a damsel in distress.

"You need a ride, Fi?"

"Yes. God, yes."

"I thought you were on a date. Where is he?"

"Gross, don't even remind me. Someone should crown him Head Loser. Said he went out for a smoke. Never came back. What an asshole."

"Well, it's his loss. You look nice."

"Thank you, Sean."

Sean dropped me off at home. I thanked Jesus that night for making Sean show up like that outside the restaurant. I didn't ask myself why Sean was there. But more importantly, I didn't care.

THE NEXT MORNING, my father came into my room.

"How was your date?"

I peeked out from under my covers, bleary-eyed and groggy. "Huh?"

"Fiona, how was your date?"

"Dad, could you possibly have picked a bigger loser?"

"You are too picky."

"His face was pitted. His reason for living is Final Fantasy.

I'd rather be dead."

"Fiona, what did you two do?"

"Do? I watched him slurp down his noodles. Then he left."

"You must have said something rude."

Yeah, me. Rude.

"Dad, why don't you phone Freddie's mother and ask her? I'm sure he gave her a full report. It's Monday. I have to get ready for work."

My father got up and left. I heard him outside on the phone.

"What? No, Fiona is right here. She's fine...." My father's voice trailed off. I turned over to steal five more minutes of sleep before starting my ninety-hour billable week.

But I was denied the luxury.

"Mrs. Kong said Freddie didn't come home last night."

"Maybe he finally left home and decided to get a life."

"Fiona, it's not funny. What did you do? Did you say something to upset Freddie?"

"Dad, please. Me? What could I possibly have said?"

"You probably scared him off. I told you to wear lipstick."

"Yes, Dad. That would certainly have made a big difference."

"When I showed Mrs. Kong your picture, she said that you were too dark. You need to bleach your skin and wear some lipstick. You'll look more like a lady. And whiter."

Christ. Mrs. Kong needed a major enema.

"Dad, I'm going to work."

"Not until you tell me where Freddie went."

"I don't know, Dad. He ditched me at the restaurant with the bill, no less. Yes, I had to pay for my own meal."

"What?"

"Yup."

"You had to pay?"

"Yup."

My father got up.

"To hell with them then. I'm going to tell Mrs. Kong to go to hell. And to take her cheapskate son with her."

Go, Daddy.

The boy not paying for my dinner. You get hell for that.

I REALLY SHOULD READ the news. It's good to know what's happening in your own city. If it only weren't all so depressing. But if you're meant to hear a piece of news, you'll hear about it one way or another.

"Bad news. Freddie's dead. They found his body out behind that restaurant. Someone slit his throat for his wallet," my father told me later that night.

"Really?"

I suddenly felt giddy. Asshole had it coming. I hoped that the bird-hater was rotting in hell. Maybe Satan's crows were picking out his eyes right now.

Then I remembered his pet turtle, Fei. I wondered if it would miss Freddie. I wondered who would feed Fei now, change its water, tell it that it was the best little turtle in the world. Maybe Freddie didn't tell Fei that. That would be one more reason why Freddie should rot in hell.

And then I felt bad. For Fei.

"Yes, Fi. You're a lucky girl that you were not with him outside."

"Yeah, guess I was destined to pay for my own food."

"I never liked his mother anyway. Forget Freddie."

Done. So done.

"You have another date next Sunday, Fi."

Hai, Daddy.

"And Fiona?"

"Yeah?"

"Wear lipstick."

CHAPTER
SEVEN

S EAN ALWAYS KNEW HOW to make an appearance.
At St. Sebastian's, he always waited until the last minute
before the bell rang to make a mad dash into homeroom
after recess, lunch, class change. Tom Cruise *Risky Business*-style.
He'd skid right through the door, straight into Sister Maria's desk.

"Sorry, Sister. I was finishing up penance. Twenty Hail Marys.
Five Our Fathers."

"You went to Confession at lunch, Sean?"

"Yes, Sister. I felt bad for using the Lord's name in vain. Because it hurt Jesus."

Liar.

Sean had been finishing his second cigarette out behind the
rectory. I watched him inhale his nicotine lunch. He watched me
put away my Kraft American Singles cheese sandwich.

"Cigarettes are expensive, Fi. Gotta savor each one to the
end. A cigarette is a terrible thing to waste."

"Sean, you stole those from your dad."

"Well, he had to pay good money for them. Besides, I'm doing the old man a favor. I'm saving him from early lung cancer."

It worked. Sean saved his father from lung cancer. Too bad Sean didn't drink the old man's liquor for him too.

Always thinking of others, Sean was.

"HI, FI. READY FOR a night out with your old buddy?"

Sean opened the door dressed in nothing but smooth skin and a flamingo pink feather boa looped around his neck. He had asked me to meet him at his apartment on Russian Hill before heading out for an evening of bar hopping with him in the City the weekend following my tragic date with Freddie. When I asked him why, he said, "Because I have something to show you."

Cobain's voice floated out from Sean's apartment. Another thing we had in common. Nirvana on Repeat One.

Come

As you are

As you were

"God, Sean. I think I'm too dressed for where you have in mind. Is this what you wanted to show me?"

I had donned a ruffled black D&G top with skinny Chloe jeans and maroon patent leather Dior stilettos. Bar clothes.

"Cool shoes, Fi. Nah, that's still inside. But I decided to torture you today," Sean said, fingering his feather boa dangerously.

"How so?"

"By denying you the pleasure of tearing my clothes off."

"Oh, you sadist. You hurt me so."

As I want you to be

"So you going to come in or what, Fi? No worries, I'm not going to rape you."

I rolled my eyes, wondering what Sean's neighbors thought of him. A hymen restoration surgeon with a penchant for feather boas.

"You put that away! Or I'm gonna call the cops, young man!" an undead version of Estelle Getty in a flower tea dress screamed. She must have been watching from the peephole of her apartment, across from Sean's. His attire had prompted her to step out into the hall and butt into our lives.

"Go back to your solitaire game, Betty. Or I'll call the mobile mental health unit and treat you to a night in General's psych ward," snapped Sean.

He pulled me into his apartment and slammed the door. I heard Betty gasp.

"She hasn't seen a naked man in decades, Sean. You could've given her a heart attack. Then you would've had to do CPR on her."

"Nah, last rites would be more appropriate for her condition. Too old. So you want some wine, beer, anything, Fi?"

"Water's good, seeing that we're planning to go out drinking all night."

Sean got me a glass of water.

"Ooh, Wedgwood. Nice, Sean. Where did you get that boa?"

"Thank you. Halloween. A few years back. So tell me. *This*... does nothing for you?" Sean started thrusting his naked hips at me, laughing and watching my expression.

"Nice penis. But nope, afraid not."

As a friend

As a friend

"Then why do you dress like that, Fi?" Sean scrutinized my outfit, zeroing in on my Dior stilettos.

"Because I don't think they'd let me in if I was wearing a Hefty garbage bag and Kleenex boxes for shoes."

"Good point. I wouldn't walk next to you if you were."

"See? Clothes aren't just to attract men. That and I can really hurt a man with these heels." I laughed. "Want me to kick you in the tailpipe with these?"

"Christ, Fi. No thanks. Geez, zero libido. Unbelievable. How else can you say no to *this*?"

"Are you trying to tempt me or something?"

"Duh. Fi, I'm naked and making obscene gestures at you. Hey, just so you know, I may hold my knife and fork like a hymen surgeon, but I can fuck like a tree surgeon." Sean continued to thrust his hips at me, laughing. Then he finished with some hip circles.

As a known memory

"Save it for the trees then, Sean. Just put some clothes on and let's go."

"Suit yourself. Your loss."

He sauntered off to his bedroom and closed the door behind him. But not before giving himself a hard slap on his behind. He must have suffered a sudden burst of modesty.

I had been half in love with Sean since that day he talked me into clobbering Jeremy. Half in love.

I had been half in fear with Sean since that day he lit Stephanie's head of fire and walked away without looking back.

Like with Hank's giant Argentine boa constrictor, George.

Hank used to be our next door neighbor. Sometimes after school, I would go over to watch Hank feed George. When Hank dropped in scurrying white mice, George would stir to life, pulling its massive thick body into movement.

One day, George perked up and looked directly at me, ignoring the mouse that Hank was dangling. It slid its nose against the glass, stared into my eyes, and jerked its head at me twice. There was an instant connection, an interspecies bond. Fascinated, I felt special, lucky, honored to be noticed by the snake. Unique, like Harry Potter.

I fell half in love.

George's diet included a wide variety of mammals, including birds, larger lizards, ocelots, and eventually Hank. One evening, Hank fell asleep on the couch with the snake tank open. George strangled him. Then it tried to swallow him whole, but Hank was too big around the shoulders. And George refused to let go. So it suffocated.

I fell half in fear.

Hank and George needed that separation of glass and steel to survive in the same space. That protective barrier between the species kept disaster at bay.

Like me and Sean.

Sleeping with him would be like curling up with George. Bad idea.

"And oh, check out my new toy in the other room, Fi."

Sean poked his head out and jerked it towards the right.

Take your time

Hurry up

The expensive, sleek teak furniture screamed Ethan Allen. Heavy, frosted glass coffee table with black wooden legs. Black leather sofa set. Hip, modern, chic.

But not the black and white photos of defecating zoo animals in glass box frames. Those said Sean. His statement on wall art.

And the large punching bag shaped like a giant baby hanging from the ceiling and anchored to the floor with a metal chain. I punched its swollen belly and it wailed like a cholericly newborn, sounding more and more like a stuck pig.

Sean came out clad in Dolce & Gabbana from head to toe, swinging an Armani leather jacket.

"Do you like it?"

"Sean, shut it up! What the hell is that?"

Sean picked up a baseball bat that was leaning against the wall corner. He swung at the bawling baby. Hard. Harder. Until the noise stopped.

"My new toy. It's very therapeutic. Helps me deal with any aggression I have. You have to hit it until it stops screaming. Like it?"

"Where can I get one? I need one for my office."

Sean laughed. "Great, isn't it? A must-have for new parents. Would cut down on instances of child abuse."

Always thinking of others.

"Come on, Fi. Haven't got all night." As if I was the one holding him up.

Don't be late

Take a rest

As a friend

SEAN AND I WENT TO the Oak Room at the Clift Hotel. Ritzy bar scene where the people in the paintings on the wall followed you with their eyes. Drinks were fifteen dollars a pop. No sawdust on the floor. Bellinis, Cosmos, Brandy Alexanders clasped by fingers clad in Tiffany and David Yurman rings. Overpriced drinks. Overpriced trinkets.

"See? Kleenex shoes would never have gotten us in here, Sean."

"No crap, Fi." Sean removed his Armani leather jacket and hung it carefully on the back of his chair. "What do you want?"

"Bellini. What are you having?"

"Bloody Mary." Sean grinned and winked at me before heading to the bar.

Sean came back with our drinks. He pulled out the celery stick, sucked it clean, and bit off the end. He took a sip of his Bloody Mary, studying a small group of blondes clustered around the end of the bar.

"Pick one for me, Fi."

"What are you talking about? This Bellini is awesome by the way. The hives will be worth it."

"What? What hives?"

"Oh, champagne gives me hives."

"Then why are drinking that, Fi?"

"Because it's yummy, Sean. Yuuuummmy."

Sean laughed. Sean nodded at the blondes again. "Pick one for me."

"What do you mean 'pick one'?"

"I mean pick one… for me."

"Oh I see. You are going to hit on a girl and leave me here all by my lonesome. Didn't know you liked blondes."

"I don't. Pick one. One you like the least." Sean winked.

I studied them, naming them after their drinks. You are what you drink.

Cosmo. The tallest blonde kept glancing over her shoulder at Sean, pretending to look around the room. Long, straight hair with expensive highlights. Model face. Leopard print spaghetti-strap cocktail dress. Small gardenia behind her ear. Big, acrylic French manicured nails. Louboutin stilettos. Silver Tiffany round tag charm bracelet with matching necklace.

Melonball. Cosmo's shorter companion chatted away, stirring her milky green drink every so often. She had on a paisley silk cocktail dress that was one size too small for her. Her breasts jiggled every time she waved her hand around. A hand with a large Tiffany mesh ring on the fourth finger. Prada open-toed stilettos. Silver Tiffany round tag charm bracelet without a matching necklace.

White Russian. The third blonde sat on the bar stool, nodding at Melonball's monologue. Hair pulled back into a chignon. Slinky black dress. Beaded Manolo Blahnik evening sandals. Silver Tiffany round tag charm bracelet without a matching necklace.

"Sean, they all look the same to me."

"Pick one," he said, without looking at me.

"Miss Cosmo."

"Why that one?"

"I covet her shoes. Red soles. Good luck in Chinese culture. I want her to win the lottery. That and she's so pretty." Too pretty.

Sean smiled at me. He leaned over and kissed me on the cheek. I breathed in his Aqua Di Gio.

"Yes, reminds me of someone. Look at her. Thinks she's got this whole place wrapped around her little finger."

"Well, that other one just looks boring and sad. White Russian. Bleh," I said.

Sean sipped his Bloody Mary, licking the corner of his mouth clean.

"Aren't you going to ask me what I'm going to do, Fi?"

I said nothing for a moment. Sean's eyes sparkled, daring me to ask him. Sparkled like beady serpent eyes, blinking, tantalizing, charming, lethal.

"Fi?"

"No. Should I even stick around for this?"

"Probably better if you finished your drink and went home to Pepito."

"If I was any other girl, I'd call you an asshole for telling me to finish my drink and to go home."

Sean laughed darkly. "But you are not any other girl."

Suddenly, I felt nauseous. Sick. Projectile-vomiting-punk-rock-style sick with a chill that ran down my limbs.

"Why don't we go dancing, Sean? Let's go to the Starlight Lounge."

"No. You already picked a girl for me. I have work to do. God's work."

"Forget her, Sean. Let's go dancing. Don't tell me you can't dance."

"Dancing. Someone told me once that dancing is 'the vertical expression of horizontal desires.' Wise man. And you have no horizontal desires, Fi."

"But I like the vertical expression. Come on, let's go."

"No."

"Sean. Come on."

"No, Fi. I'm busy this evening. Go home."

"Sean. Come on."

"No."

"Then take me home first. I might trip and die in these shoes. Or get mugged by some junkie."

"So kick the bastard with those stilettos. Everyone has to die, Fi. Go home."

Sean stood up and strode over to the tall blonde who flipped her hair over her shoulder and flashed him her professionally-whitened smile.

What the hell. The woman was asking for it.

Death, the great equalizer. Old, ugly, sick, poor. Young, gorgeous, healthy, rich. It doesn't matter to the Reaper. Everyone ends up the same way. Dead, naked, stinking to high heaven, leaking, falling to pieces in pieces.

It didn't matter to Sean either.

Everyone has to die. Especially the blonde and pretty.

CHAPTER
EIGHT

SEAN DISAPPEARED AFTER that evening at the Oak Room. Modern technology has made it easier for people to disappear. Cell phones. Email. Blackberries. Voicemail. Answering machines. All of which can make it seem like someone can be contacted every which way from Sunday. All of which can take a message. None of which can make the person you are trying to reach call you back. Not even the new iPhone. The limits of modern technology.

"Dr. Killroy is not in. He had a family emergency," said Sean's receptionist.

Sean's parents were dead. He had no siblings. He had no family that could have had an emergency.

"Can I take a message?" she asked.

Can you make him call me back?

No, you can't. The limits of human beings.

Office, home, cell, email. Multiple messages on each. Maybe Sean died. Or was passed out at home drunk. Or just didn't want to be found for a while. Either way, no Sean.

I suffered Sean withdrawal. Symptoms included lack of concentration, mood swings, anxiety, irritability, bloating, boredom. Boredom proved to be the most dangerous. Idleness and the Devil.

In my case, idleness and Laurie.

Man-crazy Laurie, who had just learned that the swanky bar two blocks from our office was hosting an Asian speed-dating event that evening. Single, available Asian boys. A whole bar full of them. Laurie's idea of a gold mine.

"Oh my God, we have to go, Fi!" Laurie's eyes glittered when she ran into my office. She bent and unbent her knees, trying to keep herself from jumping up and down.

"Not really my type of thing. Not into Asian boys."

"But I need a wing-woman."

"Don't you have work to do, Laurie?"

"Don't we all? But this is one of those can't-miss opportunities. You're not seeing someone, are you?"

"No, I'm still with Pepito."

"God, Fi, stop talking about that bird. You sound like a crazy bird lady. So you coming or what?"

Asian speed-dating seemed like a good analgesic for the boredom brought on by Sean withdrawal. So I said yes.

We paid twenty-five dollars a piece to get in. The bar had a two-drink minimum. They wanted those booze goggles good and thick on us. They wanted us nice, willing, stupid for the boys. They wanted us to be mouthless, clawless Hello Kitties.

"Write your name and three things that you want the other person to know about you on your name tag," said our slinky, sexy Asian hostess. Amanda Lin, according to her name tag. Black slip cocktail dress. Faux croc stilettos. Long hair all the way down to her waist, all smelling strongly of Issey Miyake.

"Three things!" Our hostess giggled and held up three, perfectly manicured fingers.

I glanced at Amanda's name tag which listed the three things she wanted men in the room to know about her:

SHOPPING

COOKING

GIVING MASSAGES ;)

I fought my gag reflex.

"Oh, what should I write? What are you going to write?" Laurie asked, scanning the room nervously.

"Dunno yet."

I looked down on my name tag. It said "Hi, I'm" with a large blank space for my name and my three things. I grabbed a Sharpie and wrote on my "Hi, I'm" tag:

NOT A GREEN CARD TICKET

NOT A MEAL TICKET

LOOKING FOR A BIG PENIS

Laurie gasped. "Fi, you're not really going to wear that, are you?"

I peeled the waxy paper away from the label and slapped the tag on my lapel, wondering what Sean would have said had he seen what I had written. "What would you need a big penis for? Total waste on you." He would probably have said something like that. And he would have been right. Sean always was.

"Or do you think it would look better on my forehead, Laurie?"

Laurie choked on her cosmo, coughing and snorting some

out of her nose. She started laughing.

Amanda, our hostess, came over, read my tag, and gave me a nasty look. "You can't wear that. Make another tag."

"But I like this one."

"No man is going to want you."

Right.

"Okay, everyone. No talking. As you all know, this is silent speed-dating. Instead of speaking, you'll be writing messages to each other on these index cards." Our host held up salmon-colored 3x5 index cards, waving them over her head. "Okay, ready? No talking from now on until I say so."

"Laurie, what is this?"

"Silent speed-dating, Fi. Shhhh!"

Save me, Jesus.

But Jesus wasn't listening.

I wrote "Hi (Duh)" on my first index card and flashed it about. Three guys walked over to me and Laurie. They looked at my name tag, laughed, and started scribbling on their pink cards.

Hi, I'm Joe. You're funny.

Hi, I'm Thomas. You're funny.

Hi, I'm Greg. You're funny.

Duh.

Laurie scribbled furiously.

Hi, I'm Laurie. I'm a lawyer. I work with Fi here.

Hi.

Hi.

Hi.

Hai.

And on it went. For two hours.

I started to wonder if any coupled happiness would result from our savage use of trees, dye, and ink. Then Joe and Thomas returned to where I was sitting at the bar. They both slipped me an index card. Each had a phone numbers scrawled on it.

Laurie smiled and waved at them. They waved back and walked away.

Her tag read, "Hi, I'm"

LAURIE WONG

SHOPPING — MOVIES — RUNNING

No phone numbers for Laurie.

Poor girl.

Laurie and I walked back to the office after the speed-dating event. We still had a busy night ahead of us. After all, ninety-hour weeks don't bill themselves.

"Fi, you did well! Wow. Two numbers. Are you going to call them?"

"No."

"Why not? It can't hurt to get to know more people. I just signed myself up on match.com and eHarmony this week. I'm waiting for my matches. You want to sign up too?"

No. I don't want to die.

Internet dating can be hazardous to your health.

Just ask Raymond Merrill. But you can't. He's dead.

All the fifty-six-year-old carpenter from San Bruno, California wanted was a woman to love. All he did was answer an ad on a Brazilian marriage website promising to make his dreams come true.

I wonder if his dreams ever included being kidnapped, robbed, drugged, strangled, doused with gasoline and set on fire in a vacant

77

lot in Brazil by the woman he thought was the love of his life.

Because that was what Raymond got. Poor man. Talk about being a victim of false advertising.

So I told Laurie.

"No, that only happens in rare cases. You met Joe and Thomas in person first."

So obviously they could not turn out to be psychos later.

"Besides, just have them take you to a movie or something. Keep it near your house so if anything weird happens, you can just leave, Fi."

True. Laurie had a point. But I wasn't interested in Joe. Or Thomas.

"At least you got some numbers," said Laurie wistfully.

I felt bad. Like I owed it to poor Laurie to call one of those guys because she didn't get any numbers. So I had to date for the both of us.

We returned to our world of buy-sell agreements, schedules, exhibits, letters of understanding. The two drinks I had didn't make those documents any easier to draft, so instead, I checked my email. I checked my voicemail, my cell phone, my Blackberry.

Nothing. The world had gone Sean silent.

I took off my blazer, reaching into the pocket to clear it of any debris. Two pink index cards with phone numbers slipped into my hand.

Joe.

Thomas.

I couldn't remember what Joe looked like. Thomas' face came vaguely into focus in my memory. His visage was not too unpalatable. Perhaps if I squinted really hard, I could turn him into a Chinese Ryan Phillippe. Probably not.

My cell phone rang.

"Fiona? It's Dad."

Duh.

I saw my home number flash thanks to Caller ID. The beauty of modern technology. You can now tell who is trying to reach you so you can decide whether or not to hang up on them. You no longer have to lie and say that you have something burning on the stove. Or pretend that you have to move your bowels. Modern technology gives a helping hand to morality, saving us all from the hell fires reserved for liars.

"Are you still working at the office?"

"Yup. Billing away, like a good little associate."

"Good. I have good news. I set up another date for you this weekend. He's the son of the head chef at the best restaurant in Chinatown."

Son of a chef. Great. Probably fat and spoiled by professional cooking. But I was too tired to argue with my father. And I knew it would be useless. He would just give me the silent treatment until I agreed to go. You rebel, you get shut out. I'd learned that lesson at Uncle Yuen's house.

"Everything tastes the same in Chinatown. Which one?"

"The one with the glass doors, Fiona."

All the restaurants in Chinatown had glass doors.

"Oh, that one, Dad."

"He's a great boy. You'll like him."

"But Dad, I can't go."

"Why not? Can't you take a day off this weekend?"

"No, it's not that, Dad. I have a date," I lied.

"What?"

"Date, Dad. Date. With a man. Chinese man."

"Really? When did you meet him?"

"Tonight. Laurie dragged me to an Asian speed-dating event. I met someone."

"What does he do for a living, Fiona?"

"Computer engineer. UC Berkeley grad."

"UC BERKELEY?!"

"Dad, don't yell. I have a headache."

"Have you been drinking?"

"No," I lied.

"Are you drunk, Fiona?"

"No. God, Dad."

"This boy is real?"

"Christ, Dad. Yes, we are going to a movie this weekend."

"Wow. He really went to UC Berkeley?"

"That's what he said, but he could be a big fat liar."

"What is his name?"

"Thomas Lam," I said, reading the jagged handwriting on the index card.

"Okay, I'll change your date to the following weekend."

"What?"

"You can't put all your eggs in one basket, Fiona. Especially you."

Especially me. Who couldn't hold a man, with or without a missing hymen.

"Dad."

"Did Thomas really go to UC Berkeley?"

"I don't know, Dad. I told you. That's what he said."

"Okay. Go back to work. I'll take care of your other date. You go on this one first. And remember. Wear lipstick."

Hai.

UNIVERSITY OF CALIFORNIA at Berkeley. UC Berkeley. CAL.

For Chinese-Americans living in Northern California, UC Berkeley is Harvard, Yale, Princeton, Columbia, Stanford, Cambridge, Oxford all rolled into one. High school kids have killed themselves upon getting rejected by UC Berkeley. Your life is worthless if UC Berkeley does not deem you worthy of acceptance.

Getting in and graduating from UC Berkeley means that you can walk down the street sideways. You will be hailed as a genius. You will be successful. You will be an engineer, a doctor, a millionaire. You will marry the right person and live in the perfect house in the Sunset District and have two boys. You will be set for life.

For life.

That is the UC Berkeley promise.

Never mind that I had gone to Yale. The fact that Thomas had gone to UC Berkeley impressed my father. He and my mother were probably making my wedding plans for me right now.

Too bad I didn't have a date with Thomas. I had no intention of setting one up with him. It was just easier to lie than to argue with my father during the onset of a major migraine. After I got off the phone, I checked my voicemail, Blackberry, email again.

Two new messages were highlighted in bold in my Gmail inbox.

One was an offer to sell me Viagra at a discount.

The other was a call to join a campaign to save the wolves. Apparently, the wolves needed saving.

And a Gmail ad alerted me that Hello Kitty underwear was forty to sixty percent off at Overstock.com.

No Sean.

Idleness and lack of Sean.

Idleness and Thomas.

I picked up the pink index card with Thomas' number. I propped it up next to my phone to remind me to call him tomorrow. What the hell. I could always bring my pepper spray and butterfly knife along. Good date companions.

Raymond Merrill should have brought his.

FLUNITRAZEPAM, OR WHAT a news anchor calls Rohypnol, or what your average date rapist calls a roofie, makes a great date companion.

Sean tossed a couple of tablets in a little plastic bag at me.

"Take these with you. In case you need to knock him out."

"Sean, I'm not planning to rape or rob him."

"No, but in case you need to make an emergency getaway. Induces anterograde amnesia. Residual amounts in the body almost impossible to detect. Perfect drug."

"Anterograde amnesia?"

"Means he won't remember anything after you knock him out. He'll remember everything before."

"Ah. Cool. But I already have pepper spray and a knife. I think I'm good to go, Sean."

"Pepper spray is dangerous. You gotta pay attention to what direction the wind is blowing or you end up with it in your own face. Stupid. Who pays attention to that when you're being attacked?"

Sean had a good point.

"And leave the knife at home, Fi. Makes you look guilty. Carrying a concealed weapon. Assault with a deadly weapon. You'll just get yourself in trouble. Geez, you're the lawyer. Don't you know that stuff?"

Sean was right.

"Besides, if you need to use a weapon, always use something that belongs to him. Wipe off your prints. So it doesn't get traced back to you, Fi."

Always thinking of me, Sean was.

SEAN CALLED ME the evening after I had made a date with Thomas. He invited me over to his apartment for drinks on Friday night. This time, he answered the door wearing clothes. Normal clothes. I wondered if Betty was disappointed.

"Where the hell have you been the last few days, Sean?"

"I needed to take care of something."

Sean looked at me and smiled. Smiled like he did the day they took him away, after he set Stephanie on fire. He paused, daring me to ask him what anyone else would have asked him. "What? What did you have to take care of?" But I wasn't anyone else.

So I didn't.

Like I didn't ask him why he had roofies in his possession.

That was one of the first lessons I had learned in evidence class at law school. Never ask one question too many.

The most famous example given by Professor Fossett involved the cross-examination of an eyewitness to an assault and battery by an unfortunate defense attorney.

"Sir, did you actually see the defendant bite off Mr. Smith's ear?"

"No, sir."

"Then how do you know that he was the one who bit off Mr. Smith's ear?"

"Because when I turned around, I saw him spit it out."

One question too many could cost you your case. Or your life. So I changed the topic of conversation.

"Well, you missed a whole lot of excitement. Laurie dragged me off to an Asian speed-dating event. I have a date tomorrow with a nice Chinese boy. Thomas. Went to UC Berkeley."

"Your Dad must be thrilled."

"He is. I wasn't planning to actually go out with the guy, but then my father called and told me he had another date set up for me. I figured Thomas would be better than whatever he had in store."

That was when Sean tossed the packet of roofies at me. After we chatted about the benefits of roofies and the liabilities of my knife, Sean said, "Fi, I got you something. Thought you would like it."

Sean walked to his dining table, picked up something, and gave it to me.

"Here, wear this behind your ear. It's all the rage now."

It was a small gardenia. Miss Cosmo's.

I didn't ask him why. I just thought about the lawyer who lost his case by asking one too many questions.

The next day, I found myself waiting for Thomas at the Sony Metreon, San Francisco's modern-day watering hole, entertainment arena, and shopping mall. My pepper spray and Sean's roofies were safely tucked in my purse. Thomas and I had planned to see the two o'clock movie. My watch read a quarter to three.

"I'm still trying to find street parking," said Thomas, fading in and out on my cell phone. His English carried a heavy Cantonese accent. Damn silent speed-dating.

"Thomas, it's Saturday afternoon in downtown San Francisco. You are not going to find street parking. Park at the Yerba Buena Parking Garage. It's right across the street from the Metreon."

"Oh, I know. But that's expensive."

I should have left the theater at that point. What a cheapskate. What a loser. Any man who would make his date wait forty-five minutes while he tried to find street parking deserved to be kicked in the groin. Or worse.

I called Thomas back.

"Look, I don't have time for this bullshit. I'm leaving."

"No, I'm so sorry. I just found parking. I'm walking into the theater now."

And he was.

Thomas. Five foot nine inches. Collared shirt. Leather bomber jacket. GAP khaki pants. Black leather shoes.

"I'm so sorry, Fiona." He gave me a huge bear hug, smelling like CK One.

"Well, the movie's half over. And I'm hungry. I want to eat."

"Uh, I already ate. I'm not that hungry."

Yeah, right. The cheap bastard probably just didn't want to pay for a meal.

"Well, I want to eat."

"Oh okay. What do you want?"

"I want Japanese. Let's go to Sanraku."

"You like Japanese? Why don't we go to Japantown? Actually, you wanna go karaoke?"

Karaoke.

Which literally means "tone deaf." Invented by Daisuke Inoue to provide "an entirely new way for people to learn to tolerate each other." Because you have to be tone deaf, drunk, or dead, to stand it. And not kill your friends for partaking in it. Modern technique for teaching toleration.

But it's the drug of choice for young Asians everywhere. It's the mahjong for the forty and under. Belting out songs off-key at the top of your lungs in a cramped, windowless booth in front of a glaring television screen with nothing but booze to keep you going. Asians call it entertainment.

I call it late twentieth century's answer to the rack. A hi-tech version of fingernails down a chalkboard.

And it made me think about Thomas in an "entirely new way" as he bellowed ABBA songs into the microphone, right next to my ear.

"See that girl, watch that scene, dig in the dancing queen..."

Thomas put his arm around my shoulder and took another swig of beer.

"Come on, Fiona. Sing with me," he said, thrusting the microphone in front of my face.

My stomach growled. We never went to get food. I am hypoglycemic. So I always carry a couple of Nature Valley granola bars in my purse. Apple and cinnamon crisp. Raisin and almond.

Thank God for granola bars.

"You are the dancing queen, young and sweet, only seventeen…"

On dates, most people wonder what the other person looks like naked. What her boobs look like. How big his penis is. If he's good in bed. If she's into anal. If he snores. And how many dates it would take to get her into the sack.

I found myself wondering how Thomas was going to die. And what he would look like as a corpse. People always look different when they're dead. They don't look the same as when they're screeching out the lyrics of "Eternal Flame."

I wished Sean was there.

And then I realized he was. In two white tablets.

Thomas took a break while he waited for the next song on the queue to load. He guzzled more Sing Tao beer.

"This dating thing is sorta new to me, Fiona. I haven't really dated before."

"Really? You're joking. How old are you?"

"I'm thirty-five."

"What the fuck?"

"Sorry, is that weird?"

"No, man, that is scary. Creepy. What's wrong with you?"

"Oh, well, I just focused on my career a lot. I went to UC Bookaley." UC Berkeley. Pronounced UC Bookaley by little old Chinese ladies who only spoke a few words of English. Not a UC Berkeley grad.

"Thomas, were you born here?"

"Oh yes, I was born in San Jose actually."

Asian Grand Central. No wonder. An American-born Chinese with a Cantonese accent.

"You're an engineer, right?"

"Well, I got my degree in engineering, but I'm a project manager for a hi-tech company in Menlo Park."

"So you've never had a girlfriend?"

"No, I dated someone in high school once. But that was for senior prom."

Holy crap.

I felt less absurd, thinking of Mr. Happy and my bottle of Lidocaine. Here was someone who had been living in a cave, a Silicon Valley cave.

"Why haven't you dated, Thomas?"

"Like I said, I just focused on my career. You went to Yale, right?"

"Yeah."

"Wow. That's so cool."

"Thanks. So why are you dating now?"

"Oh, my father said that it was time for me to find someone and get married. Oh, here comes the next song. It's one of my favorites. I love this one."

"Love Shack," by the B-52's.

"Cool, Thomas. Here, let me get you another beer."

And I did.

I'm headin' down the Atlanta highway,

lookin' for the love getaway

Heading for the love getaway

Thomas never got to scream out the best part of the song. The part that went *"Love Shack, baby Love Shack! Love Shack, baby Love Shack!"*

So I did it for him.

Too bad he didn't hear me. At least I was on key.

Poor Thomas.

"I'm stepping out for some air. My boyfriend is still in there. He'll take care of the tab," I said to the attendant outside.

An emergency getaway. A love getaway.

Sean was right.

My father accosted me at the door when I got home.

"Well, how did your date with Thomas go?"

"Forget it, Dad. He was a loser."

"So picky, Fiona. Did he really go to UC Berkeley?"

"Yeah, got his engineering degree. But he's not an engineer. Project manager for some hi-tech company."

"He's in computers then."

"I don't know, Dad. Total loser."

"Why?"

"Big cheapskate."

"You spend too much money."

"Dad, he was forty-five minutes late because he was looking for street parking."

"Oh, how practical. So he's a frugal boy."

"Dad, he didn't want to buy me lunch. He said he had already eaten."

"What?"

"Yeah. He didn't want to pay for food."

"Tell him to go home to his mother."

"I did."

"Good. I set you up with Don for next Saturday afternoon. Dim sum. You'll like him. His father is a chef."

"Yes, you already told me that, Dad. I'm really not interested."

"How do you know? You haven't even met him yet."

"Does he speak English?"

"Yes, of course he speaks English."

"With or without a Chinese accent?"

"He was born here, Fiona."

"So was Thomas. He had an accent."

"Oh. Well, no. I don't think he has an accent. You'll like him."

"Whatever, Dad. I'm going to take a shower."

"Next Saturday, Fiona."

"Yeah, I know. I'll wear lipstick."

I needed more roofies.

CHAPTER
TEN

O N MONDAY MORNING, the LLP in Toller & Benning LLP took on a new meaning. Land of Laid-Off Persons. The firm told me and eighty-four other associates that the quality of our work plummeted below firm standards overnight. And sent us packing with one banker's box each.

Jack told me over the phone even though his office was less than fifty feet away.

Nice man, Jack was.

"Sorry, Fi. Your performance has been mediocre lately and we are going to have to let you go."

"But Jack, you gave me top ratings three months ago at my last performance review."

"Yeah, three months ago. You have to keep the quality of your work up."

"You praised the Purchase and Sale Agreement I drafted for Hexcon, Inc. just last week."

"Wake up and smell the crap. It's everywhere. Read your

own timesheet."

Jack was right.

I had billed only twenty-five hours last week. Most of the entries read:

Prepare mailing list for shareholder notifications. 5.0

Arrange, coordinate, and manage shareholder notification mailing. 4.3

Confirm notification mailing. 2.0

I guess the client no longer wanted to pay me to type up address labels, fill out FedEx mailing forms, and spend two hours double-checking each package tracking number with FedEx on the phone. All at two hundred and seventy-five dollars an hour.

Who could blame them?

Layoffs. Downsizing. Performance cuts. Or what law firm management calls "normal attrition based on performance reviews." It's legalese for dumping associates when business takes a nose dive. When there isn't enough work for associates to churn out those eighty billable hours every week.

Hence, performance-related dismissals.

No one was more distraught about the news than Laurie.

"Fi, it's not fair! I had been getting top-rate reviews every year!"

"Laurie, we're not the only ones. Eighty-three more of us are marching out in a couple of hours. It's a massive layoff. No work. No profit. No associates."

"But I pulled all-nighters."

"All-nighters for licking envelopes. No one is going to pay the firm two-seventy-five an hour for us to stuff envelopes. Come on, pack your stuff."

"I have too much stuff."

Laurie sank down into her chair and sobbed. She did have

too much stuff. Framed Ansel Adams posters. Deal cubes. Two silver sansevieria plants. Books, books, and more books. Mugs, photos, lotions.

"We'll need you to vacate the premises in two hours," Jack said.

Two hours. Get your shit and get out.

I didn't have much in my office. Spartan. My décor of choice. Not one personal item, except for a box of Kleenex. I left it. And Ted Bundy with the gallery of noted miscreants on my computer desktop. I walked out with my Louis Vuitton purse. Like I was going out to lunch.

I wanted to tell my secretary, Tiffany, that I was going out for coffee. But her cubicle stood empty, along with the front desk. She, along with fifty-eight other staff members, including the receptionist, had been summoned into a conference room that morning. They never returned to their work stations.

I called Sean and whined about losing my job. He invited me over for drinks. When I arrived, he handed me a scotch on the rocks.

"I can't drink that, Sean."

"Sure, you can. You pour it into your mouth. Like this."

Sean took a swig of his scotch. I followed suit, wincing as the alcohol burned my throat.

"At least you didn't get canned for having a bum uterus, Fi."

"Or for not having a hymen, right? Yeah, that definitely would have sucked worse."

"See? There you go."

It was true.

One San Francisco firm had kicked an Asian-American associate out after she suffered a miscarriage. Six days after she got her uterus scraped, they told her to get the hell out. In one week, Hello Kitty lost her baby and her job. The legendary humanity of big law firms at its finest.

No one wanted a Hello Kitty with a defective uterus. Or worse, a Hello Kitty with one that worked properly, churning out more baby kitties, stealing away valuable billable time from the firm. Yes, that was much worse.

"At least you have your parents, Fi. Have you told them yet?"

"No, not yet. And I'd really rather not, but there's no avoiding it. But yes, thank God for them. Or I'd be out on my ass."

"No, you'll get unemployment. Can't buy Dior shoes with that though."

"Shoes are the last things I need right now, Sean. What I really need is another job."

Sean tilted his head and closed his eyes. His thinking stance.

"Fi, where do young associates go to hang out after work in your area?"

"What?"

"Bar. What bar?"

"A lot of them go to Harringtons, or the Wine Table."

"The Wine Table. Is that the fancy one that just opened up at your complex?"

"Yup. And it's expensive. I'm not going. I like your alcohol. It's free."

"Get up. We're going to the Wine Table."

"No," I said, shaking my head. "No way."

"You said you needed another job, right?"

"Yeah, so?"

"So, let's go get you one."

"One what?"

"Job. Christ, Fi. Wake up."

Sean winked at me. He took my glass, grabbed my hand, and pulled me up off his couch. He glanced at my Armani suit and nodded.

"Perfect," Sean said.

AT THE WINE TABLE, Sean and I crept into a discreet corner booth and ordered two glasses of wine. Thirty or forty young professionals were gathered around the bar, vying for attention from the pretty bartender and each other. Men and women dressed in Tahari suits, Zegna ties, Pink shirts, Prada heels, Bruno Magli loafers. Young, successful, moneyed America getting drunk after a hard day at the office.

"Which one looks like a young associate, Fi?"

"What?"

"I said, which one looks like a young associate?"

"At a law firm?"

"Yes, Fi. Are you still drunk?"

"Kinda."

"Pay attention. You want to work at a law firm, right?"

"Oh no, Sean. Associates don't have that kind of clout. I have a better chance answering ads in *The Recorder*. In fact, I should be at home right now doing just that, even though I doubt there are any immediate openings."

"That's not what I meant. Just tell me which one."

Sean stared at me, waiting. I stared back, knowing what he was thinking, but wishing I didn't. I started to feel sick.

"No, no, Sean. Let's just sit here."

"Do you want a job or not?"

"Of course, but…"

"Then tell me which one."

Sean smiled, grabbed my hand, and kissed it.

"Please, Fi, be a good girl and tell me which one. The night's not getting any younger. And I'm bored."

Sean's charm was absolute, undeniable, irresistible. And he was right. I really did need a job. And the market wasn't getting any better.

So I scanned the bar, searching for someone who looked like an overpaid mid-level associate. A handsome young man with wavy blond hair caught me looking at him. He glanced back, then averted his eyes to his friend. Late twenties, early thirties. Fit. Dark wool suit, Hugo Boss tie. Onyx cufflinks.

I kept staring at him. He looked at me again, and then turned away.

The classic bar brush-off. Not pretty enough. Not his type. Not worth his time chatting up. Not worth a drink. Because he could have anyone he wanted.

A sudden wave of resentment and jealousy gripped me. I hated the smug stranger. Because he would never have to stand out in the rain for taking a drumstick. Because he was just plain freer than I would ever be. So I told myself that I didn't pick him. He picked himself. I nudged Sean and pointed.

"That one."

"What makes you think he's an associate?"

"He's got the I'm-such-hot-shit-now-because-I-bill-out-at-two-hundred-and-seventy-five-dollars-an-hour look. I know. I had that same look once."

"The please-give-it-to-me-because-I'm-so-asking-for-it-look."

"Yup."

"Cool. Finish your drink and go home, Fi."

I raised my glass, following his direction, but paused. "Wait, but … he's a guy."

"So? You think I can only work women?" Sean's eyes glinted at me dangerously.

Oy vey.

Okay. Have a good night at work, Sean.

And I left.

"ARE YOU DRUNK, Fiona?" asked my father, when I stumbled up the stairs to my bedroom.

"Yes, I am. Very."

"Drinking? You've been drinking? How are you going to go to work tomorrow?"

"I'm not, Daddy. Got laid off today."

"What?"

"Laid off, Daddy. Lost my job today. I'm going to bed."

"Why?"

"Because business is bad."

"Were you not working hard enough?"

"Not enough work. Business is bad. No work."

"Were you drinking at work, Fi? Did you get fired for drinking?"

"What? No, Dad. I got laid off. Laurie got laid off. So did eighty-some-odd associates."

"But not everyone got fired."

"Nope, just us."

"What are you going to do, Fiona?

"First, I'm going to go to bed. Tomorrow, I'll look for another job."

"You must have done something bad."

I sighed, letting all the stale air out of me.

"Yes, I was very bad, Dad. I wouldn't wear lipstick."

"Fiona, don't be cheeky. Go to bed."

Hai, Daddy.

THE NEXT DAY, SEAN called me at home during what normal working people called lunch hour. What the unemployed called nap hour.

"There's a job opening at Beamer & Hodgins. Apply now."

"What?"

"Christ. Have you read the news, Fi?"

"No, I hate the news."

"You really should keep up with the news. Go online. SF-Gate.com."

Sean hung up.

I rolled off the couch, turned on my computer, and logged onto the Internet. The blessed Internet, the World Wide Web, my connection to the world itself.

The Breaking News tab on SFGate.com featured an article entitled:

> **Local Attorney Died Drinking:** David Keener, 30, of San Francisco died yesterday evening at the Wine Table, the new, trendy Downtown bar after consuming a large quantity of alcohol and unknown sedatives. Keener was discovered after he passed out in the restroom by another patron. He was pronounced dead at the scene when the paramedics failed to revive him after repeated attempts. Keener was an associate in the corporate and securities group at the prestigious San Francisco law firm of Beamer & Hodgins LLP.

The article continued with a trite discussion about binge drinking being an occupational hazard of the law profession, how young associates turned to the bottle after toiling through ninety-hour billable weeks and enduring abusive senior partners, how law firms needed to reexamine the culture and environment in which they operated, how senior attorneys needed to set better examples.

None of which mattered to me.

I logged onto Beamer & Hodgins' web site and searched for David Keener, hoping that the IT department had not yet deleted his profile from the firm directory. Keener's profile popped up, along with his firm photo.

The pixilated image smiled insipidly at me. I recognized the dark wool suit, the perfect wavy blond hair, and the Hugo Boss tie.

I did what anyone would do. I drafted a cover letter and updated my resume. I researched Beamer & Hodgins and its corporate and securities department. And Keener's senior partner. Jack Betner. Another Jack. Also white, also old, also with the I'm-such-an-asshole look.

Same shit, different toilet.

I emailed my cover letter and resume directly to Jack. Then I clicked onto the firm bios to learn about the other associates in the corporate and securities group. One girl looked almost exactly like Laurie. Face like a pie. Rimless glasses.

I typed Keener's name into the search box again.

NO RESULTS MATCHING YOUR SEARCH CRITERIA.

Half a day. Keener had been dead half a day. Beamer & Hodgins LLP had deleted him in less than twenty-four hours. The IT guys had made good use of their lunch hour. Clean, cold, efficient. My kind of firm.

Sean was right.

Beamer & Hodgins LLP had a job opening.

CHAPTER
ELEVEN

A N EMPTY OFFICE IS BAD for business. Law firms pay a lot of money to rent fancy digs to impress the clients. And when there isn't an associate sitting in an office billing furiously, the firm loses money. Lots of it.

An empty office also makes other associates uncomfortable. It's like a slight hiccup in the world of bi-weekly big paychecks, graded pay scales, set bonuses, unlimited Westlaw legal research, unlimited pens, paper clips, legal pads, Post-It notes, unlimited Alhambra drinking water.

David Keener's death gave Beamer & Hodgins LLP the hiccups.

Jack Betner knew that.

Jack needed to fill Keener's office with a warm body. Any warm body with a J.D. from a decent school who was willing to put up with his crap and bill ninety hours a week in exchange for a six-figure salary.

A warm body like mine.

"So do you golf, Fiona?"

"No, Mr. Betner, I do not."

"It's Jack. And good. Means you'll be here every weekend instead of out farting about on the golf course."

No, I'll be going on arranged dates orchestrated by my father instead.

But it was a trick question, typical in a law firm interview. No way to know what answer Jack wanted.

And it really didn't matter.

Either way I answered the question, Jack already knew what he was going to say. It's a hallmark of a great lawyer.

Oh good. I'm a big golfer myself too. What's your handicap?

Or

Oh good. Means you'll be here every weekend instead of out farting about on the golf course.

His call. He opted for the latter as he needed to put someone in Keener's office.

"Okay, you'll be talking with Steve next, Fiona."

Round robin interviews. That's how they do it in big firms. You get passed around from associates to partners to associates to anyone who's free. People you'll be working with in your department. People you'll never see again in your life. Everyone will get a chance to drill you with silly questions and to decide whether you'll be what they call a "good fit" for the firm.

"Good fit" should mean whether you are competent to do the work required for the position. Whether you are a good lawyer. A smart lawyer.

But it doesn't.

"Good fit" means exactly that. Whether you'll fit in with

the established crowd. It's like going back to high school all over again. You're getting interviewed to join the Goths, the Geeks, the Posers, the Jocks, the In-Crowd.

Firms don't like Outcasts. They are not a "good fit."

"So what do you like to do, Fiona?" asked Hannah, a first-year associate.

"Salsa dancing, when I have time. And flying."

"Flying? Oh my God, you're so daring."

Yes, flying. I zip around in a two-seater Cessna at an airspeed of one hundred twenty knots per hour five thousand feet above the ground and my father sends me off with "have a good time." I guess the thought of me nosediving into the earth at terminal velocity in great balls of fire wasn't as bad as some boy playing with my vagina. Go figure.

"That's so cool. You sound fun. We like fun people here. We want someone fun," continued Hannah.

Something exotic. Something expensive. Something fun. Something the firm can brag about.

Our lawyers are also pilots, skiers, dancers, sailors. We're a well-rounded firm. Our associates do well enough to take flying lessons and go sailing on the weekend. Even though the associates will probably never do any of that together. Even though no one has time to do anything because they are billing one hundred hours a week. And end up dead tired. Or just dead.

What kind of hobbies do you have? Where do you live? Do you like the city? What high school did you go to? Do you like to drink? Do you like to dance? Do you golf? Do you work out?

No one asked whether I knew anything about purchase and sale agreements or venture financing. No one asked what happened at Toller & Benning LLP. No one asked whether I had even passed the bar. No one asked how I knew they had a job opening in their department.

It didn't matter.

They just wanted someone fun to cure their hiccups.

On Friday, Jack called me.

"Fiona, everyone liked you. Can you start on Monday?"

Yes, Jack.

Of course I can, Jack.

Anything you say, Jack.

I CALLED SEAN, BUT he was in the operating room, repairing a hymen. Making his living. Salvaging a woman's ruptured honor. Doing God's work. And most importantly, putting food in the mouth of his porcupine puffer.

So I left him a message.

"Sean, name a restaurant. Dinner's on me."

"Who are you taking to dinner?" asked my father. My parents always listened in on my phone conversations. One of the disadvantages of living at home, made up for by the delicious home-cooking.

"Oh, I got a job at another firm, Dad. I'm going out to celebrate with an old friend."

"A man?"

"Yes, but he's just a friend. From law school."

"Oh, what is he?"

"He's white."

"Is he your boyfriend?"

"No, Dad. Just a friend."

"You should eat something before you go to dinner."

"But I'm going out to dinner."

"You don't know that yet. Eat something."

So I ate some oatmeal and fruit. And lucky I did. When Sean called me back later that evening, it was way past dinner time.

"I take it you got the job then."

"I did. They called me earlier. I'm starting on Monday."

"Awesome, Fi. Buy yourself some new shoes."

"Well, before that, I want to buy you dinner. But it's kind of past dinner time."

"Nah, it's okay. I already ate. Let's go do something else to celebrate."

"Like what? I do have a date tomorrow."

"Hm. Okay. Do you know where South Beach Harbor is, Fi?"

"Sure, it's next to AT&T Park. Where all the little sailboats are. Why?"

"Meet me at Gate E at noon on Sunday. Bring food and drinks."

"Ooh, are we going sailing?"

"You ask too many questions, Fi. Just bring food and drinks. Preferably finger foods. See you then. And have fun on your date tomorrow."

Another eating date. At least it wasn't karaoke.

On Saturday afternoon, I had dim sum with Don, son of a chef. And the chef himself. And his mother, his grandmother, his aunt, his little sister. And my parents.

Everyone wanted to check out the potential new member of the family. To make sure that he and I were both were Chinese. And ensure that there would be no premature hymen destruction.

No need for pepper spray, knives, or roofies.

Don was fat. Porky fat with a badly-groomed goatee and pimples. Five foot ten. Thirty years old. Home done crew cut, probably by his mother. Short-sleeved plaid shirt and jeans. Dirty sneakers. He had not troubled to make himself look nice for the big occasion.

Maybe he wanted me to like him for him. Laurie's game plan.

"So what do you like to do, Don?" I asked, trying to make some polite conversation.

Don helped himself to shrimp dumplings, avoiding all eye contact.

"Dunno. Not much. I work on my car a lot."

"You race?"

"No, I just like to work on my car. Soup it up. Looks hella good, you know."

"I'm sure it does. What else do you do?"

"Not much. Hang out at people's houses. Not much else to do in San Bruno."

"So why don't you come up to the City?"

"Nah. Nothing to do here in the City."

"But there's a lot more than what you have in San Bruno."

"Doesn't matter. All my friends are married. No one to do stuff with."

"So come up to the city and make new friends, man."

"Nah, but sometimes I like to go crabbing with my friends."

"Crabbing?"

"Yeah, catching crabs."

Okay.

I stuffed myself with some spring rolls to fill the awkward silence. No one else said anything. They were watching us converse, get to know each other, make first impressions, sniff each other's asses, paw the ground, circle around. Like zoo animals in a cage.

Don scratched the corner of his nose with his pinky, a pinky with a long, pointed fingernail. I shuddered.

Chinese boys and long fingernails. What Americans call the coke fingernail.

But it has nothing to do with drugs, and everything to do with an ancient Chinese superstition. If your pinky finger doesn't reach the farthest joint line of your fourth finger, you are destined to be poor. For life.

So Chinese folks let their pinky nails grow out. Long and pointy to ensure wealth and prosperity.

Five thousand years of Chinese wisdom and logic came up with that idea. The same logic that made using deodorant and shaving your legs and armpits taboo. Which was why my mother always hid my Degree for Women and my Gilette Satin Care shaving gel. My unmentionables.

"Mom, where did you put my deodorant? Where's my razor?"

"Not so loud, Fiona," she whispered.

"Where's my stuff, Mom?" I said louder.

"Underneath the bathroom sink. I hid them away for you."

"Why?"

"Shame."

"What?"

"Shame. If people see them, they'll think you smell and have hair, down there. I don't know why you use those things."

Because if I didn't, I would smell and have hair, down there and everywhere else.

"Mom, it's just shaving cream."

"For people who have hair."

Christ. Asian logic. Chinese mental gymnastics. Two somersaults and an Arabian flip and you're not even close to there, wherever there is.

Only people who have body odor use deodorant. So if you don't use deodorant, you don't have body odor.

Only people who have hair shave. So if you don't shave, you don't have hair. Leg hair, armpit hair, pubic hair. Shameful allusion to pubic hair.

Shame.

"So what do you like to do?" asked Don's father.

"Oh, lots of things. I started flying lessons last year. I like to drive around the city too. Clears my head."

"But those are boy things."

Boy things. Not Hello Kitty things.

"She's tuned out," said Don, like I wasn't sitting there.

"Tuned out?" I asked.

"Yeah, to life."

Yeah, because I wasn't spending my weekends tinkering with my car and hanging out at people's houses, playing Super Mario Brothers.

"Dad, do these have nuts in them?" asked Don, who had torn

a pork and spinach dumpling apart. He poked at a piece of pork with his chopsticks, turning it over to search for hidden nuts.

I stared at his plate which was strewn with bits of demolished dumpling. Then at him.

"I'm allergic to nuts."

"Oh, yeah, my son is allergic to nuts," echoed his father.

Great.

"No, no nuts," said the chef. He made these things. If anyone knew, he did.

Minus my parents, six people sat between me and what was probably my last billable-free, Don-free, Don-family-free Saturday afternoon. Six people and only one roofie tablet. I was hopelessly outnumbered. But then again, even Sean couldn't anticipate that I would need to take out a whole family.

I wondered what Sean was doing, wishing that I was with him. Anywhere but there, until Don started to die.

Don's eyes rolled back into his head. He grabbed his throat. His tongue, swollen and lumpy, poked out of his mouth like a diseased organ. A goateed mouth that looked like a vagina. He gasped for air, coughing, wheezing, spitting out a mouthful of dumpling.

"My son is choking!" Don's mother screamed.

But Don was not choking. He was dying.

"Peanuts...," Don gasped.

The wad of well-masticated pork and spinach that flew out of Don's mouth had landed on the table, a few inches from my plate. Tiny, yellow granules peppered the wet mass. Finely-ground peanuts.

The chef had been wrong about the dumplings.

"Someone call an ambulance!"

An ambulance, a doctor, an EpiPen. The chef's kingdom for an EpiPen.

Don slid right out of his chair onto the floor. His face turned a bright shade of purple, like spilt grape-flavored Kool-Aid. His mother kept slapping him on the face while his father shook his bloated, blubbery body hard from side to side, like a rag doll. His little sister pulled at his legs as he lay unconscious on the floor.

As if they could beat, shake, and pull the peanuts out of him. But the nuts were winning.

Poor Don.

Totally tuned out to life.

For life.

CHAPTER
TWELVE

SEAN'S SAILBOAT SMELLED like decomposing squirrels. During my last year at Yale, a couple of squirrels had scurried their way into an inaccessible part of the dormitory boiler room seeking warmth and shelter from a snowstorm. They starved to death, right next to the furnace.

For the entire spring semester, a heavy, sickly sweet smell permeated the air, causing headaches, vomiting, fevers. Every time I turned my head a certain way, I breathed it in. But like a too-often-worn perfume, pretty soon, I couldn't smell it anymore. After a couple of weeks, I had to run outside, draw in a deep breath of fresh air and come back inside to enjoy it again.

The sweet smell of death. Thick, toxic, intoxicating. It made me giddy. It gave me weak orgasms.

Sean's boat, *The Countess* (with the "o" curiously rubbed out), reeked of something else though, too, something that contaminated the aroma of death. It reminded me of dirty tuna cans.

"Nice name, Sean."

"Thanks, but I didn't name her. And it's bad luck to change the name of a boat. So I'm stuck with it."

"Guess you are. Sean, what on earth is that smell?"

"How the hell should I know? I can't smell anything, remember?"

Right. Thanks to the pencil Darrell shoved up your nose.

I told myself that it was the smell of the sea. And all the sea creatures that took a crap in it.

"I think it's the harbor, Sean."

Sean shrugged as he adjusted the main sail. "Here, hold the tiller and keep us on course. Aim for that little peak on Angel Island, Fi."

Angel Island. The largest island in San Francisco Bay, it is located about a mile from the Peninsula. Grass and forest cover seven hundred and forty acres of the island, which tops out at seven hundred and eighty-eight feet at the summit of Mt. Livermore, providing spectacular views of Marin County, San Francisco, the Golden Gate, the entire Bay Area.

The Miwok Indians liked it too. They fished and hunted there for over six thousand years until European settlers discovered what a great place it was to anchor and repair their ships. So the Indians had to go.

Now, it was a great place for a picnic lunch on a boat.

Sean took me sailing on his J-33 sailboat to celebrate my new job at Beamer & Hodgins LLP. Land of Lucky Persons. Grabbing the tiller, I looked up at the main sail and wished that I had gone into the hymen restoration business. No way a mid-level associate could afford to keep a boat like this.

"Christ, nice boat, Sean. I should have listened to my parents about medical school."

"And deliver babies?"

"Yeah. Something like that."

"This boat actually belonged to someone I knew."

"He sold it to you?"

"Not exactly. He died."

I didn't ask how or why. Like Sean said, everyone has to die. And you can't take it with you, contrary to what the Egyptians believed.

Dead people can't want things.

Want not, waste not.

We sailed out into the Bay, waving at everyone who cruised past us. Like polite sailors.

Everyone waves at everyone else standing on the deck of a boat. Part of proper etiquette in fish culture. It's like pilots giving other pilots the thumbs up and saying "Have a good flight" because they want to hear the same thing. No one wants to have a bad flight. And no, there's no aerosolized Prozac in the cockpit. It's just a part of bird culture.

Under the Golden Gate Bridge, a yacht sailed past. The small group of people on its deck were all dressed in black.

"Oh, look, Fi. It's our lucky day. We get to inhale the dead."

"What?"

"That yacht. *The Naiad.* It belongs to the Neptune Society. They use it to take people out here to scatter ashes at sea."

"How ironic."

"What?"

"The name, Sean. Naiad was the Greek Goddess charged with protecting life in the waters. And now she's bringing folks out here to choke her fish with death."

"Guess she got tired of her fish."

Guess she got tired of telling her fish that they were the best little fish in the world. Like Pepito was the best little bird in the world. Got tired of coddling them, protecting them.

Naiad. What a bitch.

"Do you want to be cremated, Sean?"

"Hell, yeah. Better than raising a worm farm six feet under."

"And scattered under the Bridge from the deck of *The Naiad*?"

"Fuck no. I want to be scattered in my neighborhood. So Betty can choke on me. It'll give that old girl a kick start."

Sean didn't want to be wasted on glassy-eyed fish swimming in their own muck. Always thinking of others.

We smiled and waved at the passengers on *The Naiad* a la fish culture. They didn't wave back. Rude bastards.

Sean disappeared down below. I heard him rummaging around. After a few minutes, he pulled several oddly-shaped packages wrapped in Glad garbage bags from a medium-sized cooler. He waited until we sailed farther away from *The Naiad* and shoved them over the starboard side. They bobbed on the surface for a second or two before disappearing beneath the waves.

Sean looked at me, the way a friend looks at you when he or she has just farted at the dinner table.

"Don't worry, Fi. It's all biodegradable."

That was the same thing he told Sister Maria when she caught him defecating in Father Mallory's flowerbeds next to the school-yard at St. Sebastian's. Someone had flushed a cherry bomb down a toilet in the boys' bathroom and flooded it. So as punishment, Sister Maria forced the boys to use the girls' bathroom. They had to wait until all the girls were out. But there was always one girl who had to wash her hands, fix her hair, retouch her lipgloss, smoke a cigarette.

And Sean had to go.

"When you gotta go, you gotta go, Sister."

Just ask the Reaper.

"What were you thinking, Sean?" asked Sister Maria.

"Of Jesus. Of giving back to the Earth what Jesus had given me last night at dinner. It's recycling, Sister. Don't worry. It's biodegradable."

Always thinking of Mother Earth, Sean was.

"As long as the fish find it tastier than ashes," I replied, turning my attention momentarily port side as the main sail caught a strong wind. I kept my eyes on the Angel Island peak I was aiming us toward, ignoring the packages as they slipped down into the water.

The way you pretend not to notice the smell of your friend's fart filling the room even though you can hardly breathe. People culture.

Sean's boat smelled less like dead squirrels.

Per Sean's instructions, I had brought a hefty supply of sushi, sashimi, and pot stickers. Complete with a small Tupperware full of soy sauce and wasabi. And disposable chopsticks.

Sean supplied the drinks. Water, apple-cranberry juice, vodka, and more vodka. And Jim Beam and Johnny Walker. Sean's boat was a floating bar.

"Alcohol and boating go hand in hand, Fi."

Of course they do. You have MADD. Mothers Against Drunk Driving. Not Drunk Boating. No one gets mad about that. Part of fish culture.

In Ayala Cove, we sailed past a number of boats moored at buoys. Young, tanned bodies sunbathing out on the deck, shaded by Gucci sunglasses. Drinking chilled wines in metal buckets. Nibbling on finger sandwiches. Fit, muscular bodies executing perfect dives off the bow and stern into the calmer waters of the harbor.

"Congratulations, Fi. You must have *killed* in your interview," said Sean, after we docked at a slip next to a sailboat that was much smaller than Sean's. It made his look bigger. Much bigger. Better.

Sean fixed us drinks while I laid out the food.

"Thanks. Guess they deemed me a good fit for the firm."

"Oh, I'm sure you'll do a spectacular job for whats-his-name."

"Jack."

"Jack."

Sean popped a California roll into his mouth while he studied the smaller sailboat and its occupants aboard, a March-December couple.

The sexy young Asian woman glanced at Sean, flipping her long, black hair over her shoulder before looking back at her older companion who faced away from us. Very young—like seventeen or eighteen trying to go on thirty. Salon tanned, not whitened like Cousin Katie. Long and slinky, clad in a striped bikini. Face caked with MAC makeup. Red manicured acrylic nails. She epitomized what Sean hated.

I felt uneasy, praying that she would not come over. She was pretending not to notice him staring at her with his fixed, un-nerving gaze.

"Forget it, Sean."

"Forget what? She started it."

Ten minutes later she came over, unaware of the danger. Can't blame the wolf if the lamb insists on saying hello.

"Hey there, nice boat!" she said, batting her lashes with vigor.

"Thank you," Sean replied.

The woman's companion pulled himself up from where he had been lounging on the deck and turned around to face us. I wished he hadn't.

Jack Betner. My new senior partner, clad in an island shirt with giant toucans and shorts, on his sailboat with his sweet honey.

I turned red, hoping that he would not recognize me in my polo shirt and shorts. But he did.

"She sure is a beauty," he said to Sean, referring to the boat. "Why, Fiona! Isn't this a nice surprise."

No, it wasn't.

Running into your new boss on the weekend is never a nice surprise. I would have preferred a Jack-free weekend, especially when all my future weekends at Beamer & Hodgins LLP were destined to be Jack-filled.

"Mr. Betner. Jack. Hi, didn't think I would see you until tomorrow. Sean, this is my boss at the new firm I told you about. Jack Betner."

"Hi, I'm Sean."

"Nice to meet you, Sean. Fiona, you never told me you liked to sail."

"Only when Sean has time to take me sailing."

"This is my girlfriend, Mei," said Jack, putting his arm around Mei. So Jack had an Asian fetish. He liked Hello Kitties.

"So Fiona, is this your—"

"Overprotective big brother, yes," interjected Sean.

Jack and Mei looked at me. And laughed.

"Yeah, that's right. I'm his sister. Don't you see the family resemblance?" I joked, holding out my hand to Mei.

"Of course. Absolutely," she said.

"Would you guys care for a drink? We brought way too much vodka and apple-cranberry juice. Care for a cosmo, Mei?" asked Sean.

"Oh my God, I love cosmos."

"Yes, she does," said Jack. "She'll drink you out of house and home, this one can."

"Sean, can you make me one too? I love cosmos too," I said.

"Sure thing, Sis," he replied, giving me a wink.

Sean went down below to the cooler. A few minutes later, he emerged with the drinks in his hand. He reached over the walkway and handed the drinks to Jack and Mei. Jack suddenly wrinkled his nose and sniffed at the air.

The dead squirrel smell was still there.

The sick, sweet scent of putrefaction. The smell to which I had grown accustomed on the way over to the island. The smell which faded somewhat when Sean unloaded his biodegradable cargo into the Bay, but was still discernable. My stomach lurched. I looked at Jack, the way that Sean had looked at me, like I had just farted loudly in the middle of an important client conference.

But Jack only coughed and sipped his cosmo.

"Good drink. Chopin vodka, Sean?"

"But of course. Everything else is crap."

Jack laughed, ignoring the smell of fart, the smell of death and decay. Mei giggled along, downing her drink in a few gulps.

"Sir, may I have some more?" she asked, trying to control her giggles.

"More?" Sean answered, cocking his eyebrow. "Why, yes, Oliver. Of course, you may have some *more.*" He took her cup and got up to go down to the cooler.

"Make it more part vodka, please," Mei said. "God, what is that awful smell?"

"Smell, what smell?" Sean stopped, turning around to look at her.

"Oh, honey, that's just the harbor. Probably some garbage tourists have chucked overboard. No regard for the environment, some people," Jack said. "And you probably had too much vodka. Look at you. You're all red."

And she was.

It's called the Asian flush. A little bit of alcohol, and Asians turn red all over. Like the scarlet letter, marking us for imbibing a little fun. Every drop evidenced on our yellow skin, telegraphing to the world that we can't handle our liquor.

I don't get the Asian flush. I must have a non-Asian constitution.

"No, it smells like something up and died," insisted Mei.

She had no sense of people culture.

"I don't smell it," I lied, pretending to sniff the air.

"I do. It stinks," reiterated Mei.

"Hm, I wonder what it could be. Let me get you your drink," said Sean as he disappeared into the boat with her cup.

I stood there, trying to think of something to say to fill the awkward silence. But Jack beat me to it.

"So Fiona, you excited about starting work tomorrow?"

"Oh, absolutely. I enjoyed meeting everyone in the department. Sounds like a fun group. Can't wait to join them in the trenches."

Jack laughed. "Good. Bill, bill, bill. That's what I like."

Bill, bill, bill. The mantra of private law practice.

Sean came up with Mei's drink and handed it to her over the walkway between the boats. The bright sunlight shone through the dark red liquid, making it look more like cherry Kool-Aid.

Like what Jim Jones fed to his 909 followers in Jonestown. All they wanted was to live together in harmony. All they wanted was utopia. All they got in the end was cyanide-flavored Kool-Aid.

I thought about leaping up and knocking the drink out of Mei's hand. But she was already quaffing it down. Oh well.

"That was good. I was so thirsty," Mei said, stumbling backwards. "Whoo, I think I overdid it, honey." She reached out and grabbed Jack who eased her onto the deck seat.

"Aw, sweetie. Can't hold your liquor, can you?"

"She okay?" asked Sean.

Mei lay down on the deck bench and closed her eyes.

"Oh, she's fine," said Jack.

But she wasn't.

Because she asked one too many questions. So Sean had to save his own ass.

And because she violated one of the most important tenets of people culture: You don't tell people that their farts stink. Or that their boat smells like death.

CHAPTER
THIRTEEN

"D ON WANTS TO TAKE you crabbing to make up for what happened at dim sum," my father informed me when I got home from sailing.

The ground peanuts in the dumplings had failed to kill Don properly. He survived despite their best efforts to send him back to Jesus. Stubborn bastard.

"That's okay, Dad. He really doesn't have to."

"But he wants to. He's such a nice boy."

"Dad, he's boring. And I really don't want to hang out with his entire family again."

"No, Fiona. It'll just be you two. And some of his friends."

And some of his friends. Great. His friends wanted to check out the potential future wife too.

"Tell him no thanks, Dad. I'm not interested."

"Fiona, don't be rude. He really feels bad about what happened at lunch. And his father is my friend. The least you can do is to be polite and say yes."

"Fine. Whatever."

I agreed because it was easier than arguing with my father. Been there, done that. So not doing it when I had more serious issues to deal with, like the fate of my new boss' girlfriend. I had pretended to be too full of cosmos and sushi to talk much on our way back from Angel Island. Too tired to do anything but steer us back into South Beach Harbor.

You never get into a fight with the driver when the car is travelling down a dark country road in the middle of a thunderstorm. You never accuse your friend of ruining your life or making you an accomplice to a felony when you are floating alone with him in the middle of the Bay on his sailboat. Unless you want to end up as fresh fish food.

So I waited until I was in the safety of my own bedroom to call Sean.

"Sean, tell me Mei is going to be okay."

"Sorry, Fi. Can't do that."

"Oh God. She was my new boss' girlfriend. Are you insane?"

"A little, but I like to think of myself merely as colorful."

"Not funny. Jail, Sean. Life in prison. Have you thought of that?"

"Not going to happen, Fi."

"And how do you know that, Sean?"

"Didn't you see Jack's wedding band?"

"What?"

"Wedding band, Fi. The guy was wearing a wedding band, and Mei sure wasn't Mrs. Betner."

"So he was with his mistress. So what?"

"So you think he's going to drop an underage, drunk, unconscious girl off at the ER? Think of what that would do for his reputation and his marriage."

"She wasn't underage, I don't think. She *looked* at least eighteen."

"I meant under the legal drinking age. Think of how that would play out in the papers."

"Sean, this is serious. Jack will probably report us to the police."

"No, he won't. He'll be held responsible for anything that happens to her. That and he's probably worth too much to risk his wife finding out. A divorce would kill him."

"So you think he's just going to do nothing?"

"Oh, not nothing. I think he's going to make it all okay."

"Sean, this is nuts."

"Not our fault she was drinking. And it was on Jack's boat, not ours."

"Christ, I have to see him tomorrow morning. What am I going to do?"

"Nothing, because nothing happened."

I wanted to ask him what else was in those drinks. But I didn't. Partly because of self-preservation and partly because I already knew. He had slipped a lethal dose of roofies into Mei's cosmos for carrying on about the smell of death emanating from his boat. For not adhering to the rules of people culture.

"You think Jack is that big of an asshole, Sean?"

"You tell me."

On Monday morning, I showed up early in a three-piece Tahari suit and three-inch Dior heels. Annette, the head of Human Resources, showed me to David Keener's old office.

The office windows faced the San Francisco Bay from the

twenty-first floor. The bay, the sky, the hills, the City. I didn't need wall art. The City would be my living decoration. Keener had also enjoyed a state-of-the-art computer and personal printer. Everything he needed to bill eighty, ninety hours a week at peak efficiency. Keener had it good.

"So, Fiona, how do you like your new office?"

"Jack, good morning. It's fabulous. I think I'm going to be very happy here."

"Good, good. Could you step into my office for a minute?"

A wave of nausea swept over me. I was sure that a couple of homicide detectives would be waiting for me. And of all things, on my first day on the job. It would make the front page of *The Recorder*, the legal newspaper.

But when I walked into Jack's office, it was empty, except for the mountainous piles of files, books, and papers on his desk, couch, and floor. I also noticed something I hadn't during my initial interview: a family photo on the credenza behind his desk.

A smiling photo of a late-middle-aged woman with graying curls hugging two freckled-faced women in their twenties. Jack's wife, Mrs. Betner. And their two daughters. His family. And a photo of a golden retriever, his dog.

But no photos of Mei. His mistress.

Duh.

I wanted to ask Jack if Mei was all right. But I thought better of it and allowed him to steer the conversation.

"So Fiona, how was your last weekend of freedom?"

"Relaxing and free. But I'm ready to work."

"Did you do anything fun?"

Jack put out the bait. He waited to see if I was going to bite.

"Not really. Just kicked back and spent some time hanging out with an old friend. I wanted to rest up for my big day."

"Good for you. I spent Saturday with my wife and kids. Don't get to see the girls too often now. Young people seem to have lives of their own these days. And I was here all day Sunday, working. No rest for the wicked."

He let out an uneasy laugh, and then stared at me. Hard. I got the message.

"Wow. You must be busy. Speaking of which, my assignments?"

Jack beamed. He tossed two merger agreements at me. "That should keep you plenty busy, Fiona."

Sean was right. Nothing to worry about. Jack was a total asshole. You can always count on an asshole to be an asshole.

THAT EVENING, I BEGAN my new daily ritual of reading the news. I couldn't stand news anchors with their perfect broadcast hair, makeup, and suits. Their Crest-clean smiles. The flashing logos of the television stations. The turned-up volume of commercials. So I read my news online, on the blessed Internet, on SFGate.com.

Under the news tab, I discovered an article of interest entitled:

Asian Woman Drowned in SF Bay: An unidentified Asian woman, in her late teens, was found dead early this morning in the San Francisco Bay by boaters. Police investigators believe that the young woman probably

fell off a boat and drowned after consuming a large
quantity of alcohol and unknown sedatives. Police are
searching for any possible witnesses to the incident.

The article continued with the usual discussion about heavy
drinking being a hazard of boating, how young people consume
too much alcohol these days, how parents should keep a closer
eye on the partying behavior of their children, and how police
need to crack down harder on underage drinking.

None of which interested me in the slightest.

So Jack made everything okay by tossing Mei off his boat.
No one wanted a dead Hello Kitty full of vodka and roofies. No
one but the fish.

Want not, waste not.

"See? I told you nothing would happen."

"Yeah, Sean. Looks like you were right."

"How did your first day of work go?"

"I'm still here."

"Fi, it's almost eleven o'clock."

"Uh huh. And I'm still here. Jack is keeping me very busy."

"You know what they say about idleness and the Devil."

"Yeah."

Bill, bill, bill.

That was all I knew. Nothing about a sailing trip to Angel
Island. Nothing about Jack in a toucan island shirt. Nothing about
apple-cranberry juice and vodka. Nothing about Mei.

And I also knew absolutely nothing about crabbing.

"Don's taking you up to San Pablo Bay this weekend to go
crabbing, Fiona."

"Are you serious, Dad? I'd really rather not go."

"Well, too bad. You already said yes. And I already told him."

"Dad, I have to work this weekend. New job. Don't want the new boss to think I'm lazy."

"You can take one evening off. You are leaving Friday night."

"Friday night?"

"Yes, that's what I said, Fiona."

"Oh God."

"You never know, you might like him," my mother interjected.

"I already met him, and I don't like him. I'm 'tuned out,' remember?"

"Fiona, listen to your father. Just go and have fun. You'll have something exciting to tell your coworkers on Monday."

Our lawyers go crabbing. They catch the very seafood they eat. They are well-rounded hunters, gatherers, fishermen if need be. They can negotiate, draft, and bring home their own dinners. Literally. They are worth the two hundred and seventy-five dollars an hour that you will be paying.

Crabbing in San Pablo Bay.

During my flight lessons, I often flew over the San Pablo Reservoir. Better than flying in the Mount Diablo area. No hills or mountains to create air turbulence. Nice and steady airflow over the water. A perfect place to practice pitching and turning at a steady altitude. I never realized I was flying over crabbers down below.

Crabbers like Don.

According to several fishing sites on the Internet, crabbing is basically sitting around and waiting for crabs to crawl into your trap while you play card games with your buddies. You need a suitable crab trap with about one hundred feet of rope topped with a small buoy or a white plastic bleach bottle. Either one will do. You also need to rent a boat to put the trap out where the crabs scuttle about in the water.

With that, you can catch Red Rock Crabs and Dungeness Crabs. Red Rock Crabs are smaller, have less meat and a stronger flavor. But you can keep them. Dungeness have a sweet, mild flavor and plenty of succulent meat, enough for a full meal—it's what you really want to catch. So of course, it's illegal to take or possess Dungeness crabs in San Francisco and San Pablo Bay.

But not one site told a girl what she should wear to go crabbing.

"What the hell do you wear on a crabbing trip, Sean?"

"Leave the Prada at home. That's for sure."

"Christ, it sounds like we're just going to sit around in the middle of dipshit nowhere, out by the cold water, waiting to catch pneumonia."

"That sounds about right. Jeans, t-shirt, sweatshirt, jacket, gloves. What any girl would wear on a crabbing trip."

"Shit. Why didn't the peanuts kill him?"

"Because God saved him for you, Fi."

"Remind me to thank God for that one."

Sean laughed.

"It might not be so bad. You'll get to be on the water again. You liked sailing, didn't you?"

Sure.

And so I bundled myself up in a heavy North Face down jacket, jeans, GAP sweatshirt and t-shirt underneath. No gloves. I couldn't find them. All I could find were my snowflake mittens that I had worn in the third grade.

Don drove up to my house and rang the doorbell early Friday evening. When I was halfway down the stairs, my father ran after me, yelling and waving something in his hand.

"Fiona! Fiona!"

"What?"

He handed me a tube of my mother's Mary Kay cranberry blush lipstick.

"Wear lipstick."

FOURTEEN

HENRY DAVID THOREAU wrote a whole book about how great it was to be alone with Nature, how Walden Pond was the Earth's Eye, how fabulous it was to be among the trees, how he would rather sit on a pumpkin by himself than on a velvet cushion surrounded by other folks.

Problem is, Thoreau never lived in the modern age. If he had, he might have been more like Theodore Kaczynski, better known as the Unabomber. Kaczynski didn't just write diaries about living in the forest. He wasn't just happy to sit on a pumpkin or a velvet cushion. He holed up in the woods, growing crazier by the day, until he ended up building mail bombs to kill people.

In our time, Nature has become the favorite accomplice of killers, rapists, homegrown terrorists, and other assorted nutcases. The Walden Ponds conceal the bodies and cars of their hapless victims. The lovely trees and shrubs that so thrilled Thoreau now provide ample hiding places for these miscreants, creating opportunities for ambush, mayhem, murder, and terror. Helping them do God's work.

Thoreau was lucky. He died before the modern age.

If some psycho like the Unabomber didn't get you in the woods, Nature herself would. With her fangs, her stingers, her claws, her jaws, her poisons. And her cold, her rain, her darkness, and her freezing wind. In case her other weapons failed.

It took man thousands of years to crawl out of the woods. Why anyone would want to go back and spend the weekend sleeping on the ground, I had no idea.

"Don't worry, Fiona. My friends and I bought tents. Mine is big enough for the both of us."

"Tent? What tent?"

"For camping tonight, after we set up the crab traps."

"What?"

"You know, camping."

"My dad never said anything about staying overnight."

"Didn't he tell you?"

"No."

My father never said anything about camping or sharing a tent with Don. Or spending the night in the middle of dipshit nowhere without a sleeping bag.

"Don, I don't even have a sleeping bag."

"Oh, I brought an extra one."

Great.

I hate camping.

My idea of camping is staying at Motel 6 with a working toilet, shower, and electricity. And a crappy bed with sheets and pillows to keep me off Mother Nature's dirt because I am allergic to everything. To weeds, pollen, dirt, fur, plant life, animal life, dirty dinghies, tents, and even some forms of human life like Don.

"Where are we camping anyway, Don? I thought you couldn't camp overnight in the reserve."

"No, not the reserve. We are going to China Camp."

China Camp. Four miles east of San Rafael on the shores of San Pablo Bay, China Camp State Park sits on the grounds of an old Chinese shrimp-fishing settlement that once flourished in the 1880s. About five hundred immigrants from Canton, China originally called that village home. In its golden era, the settlement boasted three general stores, a marine supply shop and even a town barber.

These Cantonese fishermen netted fish and shrimp, dried them and shipped them back to China or other Chinese communities throughout the United States. Then the State of California swooped in and turned it into a park, making it a home for a variety of wildlife, including deer, squirrels and numerous birds. So the Chinese had to go.

Except for one guy, Frank Quan, who is still fishing the waters. He's the last living descendant of the old fishing families at China Camp. More power to Frank.

Take that, Miwok Indians.

"So where are the crabs, Don?"

"Oh, anywhere on the northern flats of China Camp. You'll see. It's fun."

"Are you sure you should be out in the cold, out on the water? I heard the peanuts nearly killed you."

"Oh, I'm okay now. Sorry for what happened at dim sum."

No problem.

I rocked back and forth aboard a medium-sized dinghy with

Don and his friends, Carl and Joe. They set up crab traps in the waters of the northern flats, baiting them with chicken necks. Apparently crabs love chicken necks, and they are also easy to secure onto the collapsible metal-net boxes.

Carl and Joe threw their traps into the water, marking them with floating Clorox bottles. But Don took his time, tying his chicken necks with careful delicate knots before throwing them overboard. He had a store-bought red and white buoy. Like a serious crabber.

Carl and Joe. Our chaperones. Both Chinese. Both around five foot nine inches. Both a little stocky. Both tanned. Both into crabbing with Don.

"Is this your first time crabbing, Fiona?" asked Carl.

"Yup, pretty much."

"You like it so far?"

"Uh, sure. What do we do now?"

"Oh, we wait for the crabs to crawl in."

"No, I mean, what are we going to do while we wait?"

"Well, we usually play Hearts on the shore," said Joe.

Hearts. I should have guessed.

Hearts is an "evasion-type" trick-taking playing card game for four players. It's also known as Black Lady, Chase the Lady, Crubs, Black Maria, and Black Bitch. In high school, it was the game of choice for the math, chess, and science geeks. Clusters of these kids would sit around and play in the hallways, until some jock came by and kicked their cards away for their own good.

"Do you play, Fiona?" asked Don.

"No."

I pulled out my cell phone, praying for some reception. I

wanted to call Sean, even though I doubted that he would be inclined to drive all the way out here to save me from Hearts. But I couldn't get a signal.

"Phones don't work good out here," said Don. "Here, you can watch us play."

How exciting.

Watching Don play cards with his friends and waiting for crabs to come nibble on chicken necks. Suddenly, I missed Jack and my contracts, forms, agreements. But I only had one roofie left. And I was in the sticks.

You never drug the people who are going to give you a ride back into civilization from the boonies. Who have the extra sleeping bag, the tent, and the food.

So I pretended to be interested in Hearts for hours on end. I tried to imagine being happy sitting on a pumpkin by the lake out here with Nature. But by the time Don, Carl, and Joe decided to check their traps in the evening, all I wanted to do was execute scorched earth policy to the entire immediate area.

"Aw, man. I got nothing," cried Joe, frowning at his empty trap.

"Ooh, I got one, but it's too small. I have to throw it back," said Carl as he opened his trap, releasing the dollar-sized baby crab back into the water.

Don eagerly pulled up his trap, reeling it in from his fancy buoy. As he brought it up from the water, we heard a clamor of clacking, from the crusty legs and claws of two giant Red Rock Crabs rattling inside the metal cage.

"Woo hoo! Aw, my mother is going to love this," Don exclaimed. "She loves crabs."

"You're so lucky, man," said Carl wistfully.

"No shit. More ways than one," Joe chuckled, casting a furtive glance in my direction.

God.

I made a mental note to myself to ask Sean for more roofies next time I saw him. I made another to never go crabbing again. Ever. Not with Don, not with anybody.

After a dinner consisting of pre-made ham and cheese sandwiches packed by Don's mother, we sat around a campfire drinking beer while Don and his friends drilled me about my life and my work.

"So you're really a lawyer?" asked Carl.

"Yes."

"Do you have a law license?" asked Joe.

"Yes."

"Do you like being a lawyer?" asked Carl.

"What's not to like?"

"Yeah. Being a lawyer is so cool."

"So how did you meet Don?" asked Joe.

"My dad knows his dad."

"Oh," said Carl and Joe in unison.

"Man, I'm beat. I think I'm going to go lie down in the tent," said Don.

Carl and Joe smiled, looking at me.

"Here, go on in. I'll get you a nightcap," I said, heading to the cooler. "My mom says it's always good to have some liquids right before you go to bed."

"Aw, thanks, Fiona. That's very sweet."

Take one roofie tablet in some beer, and call me in the morning.

Good night, Don.

THE NEXT MORNING, I woke up bleary-eyed and mossy-mouthed from the lack of comfortable sleep and Colgate Tartar Control toothpaste.

"Holy crap. I slept like a log! I must have been tired." Don sported the worst bed head I had ever seen.

"Yeah, you must have been. By the time I hit the sack, you were already out," I said.

"Hope I didn't snore the whole night."

"Nah."

Joe stumbled out of his tent, arching his back and rubbing his eyes. He looked around and asked, "Has anyone seen Carl?"

"No, we just woke up," I said.

"He wasn't in the tent this morning. I wonder where he went."

"Maybe he went out for a stroll along the shore."

Don shrugged and started packing his things, making sure he had his cooler with yesterday's catch.

"I hope he's not lost or something. I'd better go and look for him," said Joe.

I smiled, thinking about what might have happened to Carl. He could have been eaten by a bear, a wolf, a mountain lion, or a Jeffrey Dahmer trying to get back in touch with nature.

"CARL!" bellowed Don. "Where are you, man?"

"Damn that guy. Where is he?" said Joe, scratching himself. "I need to shower."

So did I.

I still had yesterday's makeup on my face. My Clinique cleanser was sitting on my sink at home, promising freshness and clean pores. And I was here in the middle of nowhere with Don and his two Red Rock crabs.

"Look, Don. I really have to get going. I still need to get back to the office to do some work. A lawyer's work is never done."

"Sure, Fiona. We'll head home now."

Don wasn't so bad after all.

So we got into Don's car and headed back to civilization, to the concrete jungle, to the fabulous City by the Bay, having added a fine layer of dirt, soot, and grime to our hair, and two Red Rock crabs to the cooler in the trunk.

And having lost one Carl.

CHAPTER
FIFTEEN

O N WEDNESDAY AFTERNOON, I got an email from Don, bearing a bit of good and bad news.

> *Hey Fiona:*
>
> *Bad news. They found Carl. He's dead. Drowned near the shore. Turns out he must have slipped and fallen into the water during the night when he went out to take a piss. Crabs were nibbling on him when they pulled him out.*
>
> *Good news. My mom loved the crabs I caught. They were delicious.*
>
> *-Don*

So Mother Nature got Carl after all. On behalf of their murdered ancestors, and with a little help from beer and Carl's own stupidity, the crabs of San Pablo Bay took their revenge on him. At least he didn't fall victim to a molester or sadistic psychopath. That would have been worse. More paperwork and legwork for the police when that happens. No one blames Mother Nature when she takes a life.

At least Don's mother got a good meal out of our fatal excursion.

Sean laughed when I told him about the crabbing trip.

"I told you, Fi. Don't leave home without your roofies."

"You're absolutely right. Which reminds me. I'm out. Can I have some more?"

"Oh, of course." He chuckled again. "Poor Don. He thought he was going to have fun times with you in that tent, you know."

"Oh well."

"You going out with him again?"

"What? Hell no, Sean. I've had enough Don to last a lifetime."

"You sure?"

"Oh, I'm pretty sure."

"Cool. Come by on Friday. We'll celebrate your return from the wild."

I thought that I had seen and heard the last of Don. But I was wrong.

MY PARENTS BLOCKED my way as I headed out the door for work on Friday morning. My father's eyes twinkled with glee and excitement. My mother beamed at me.

"What?"

"So you like Don, right?"

"No."

"What do you mean, 'no'? You spent the night with him." My father looked at me with a mischievous grin.

"I had no choice. You tricked me into going camping with him."

"But you spent the night with him."

"No, I didn't."

"Didn't you two share a tent?"

"Yeah, because no one told me to bring my own tent. Because no one told me that it was going to be an overnight trip."

"So you two were in the same tent."

"Yeah, but we had separate sleeping bags, Dad. Don brought along an extra one."

"But you two slept together."

"Oh my God, Dad, I really don't have time for this. Nothing happened. We didn't have sex or anything. Don conked out right away. As soon as he hit the ground."

"But you like him, right?"

"No. Don sucks."

"Fiona, stop lying. I know you like him."

"It's okay, Fiona. Nothing wrong with liking a boy," said my mother.

"Mom, I don't like him at all. Seriously. Me no like Don."

My parents exchanged puzzled glances.

"Then why did you go on the crabbing trip with him overnight?" asked my mother.

"Because Dad pushed me into it. And he never told me it was going to be overnight."

"Oh."

Yeah. It was my father's fault. Go blame him.

"Well, guess what, Fiona. You are getting married on the twenty-eighth of next month. Your mother and I will make all the arrangements. Wear lipstick."

"What? I'm getting what?"

"Married."

"Who the hell to?"

My father stared at me, blinking his eyes in surprise. "To Don, of course."

"I'm not marrying Don, Dad! This is ridiculous. What makes you think I'm going to marry him?"

"You spent the night with him."

"Who cares? We didn't do anything. This isn't China. People don't get married just because they spent the night together. Hell, they don't get married even if they've popped out three kids together."

So glad I didn't tell my father about all my other dates. Yes, Dad, just slaving away at the office.

"Fiona, you're Chinese."

"So what? I'm in America."

"Don's father and I already agreed."

"Good. Then you can go and marry Don yourself. Or better yet, his father. I'm going to work."

I stormed out of the house and sought refuge in Jack's world, my world, the world of six-minute increment billable hours. But my concentration faltered, wandering back to the morning argument with my father, replaying it over in my mind.

It's true. If you keep watching the minute hand of a clock, it never moves. In fact, the more you stare at it, the more it seems to move backwards. Friday afternoon crawled by, second by second, as I kept checking the time like an anxious child waiting for the final bell to ring for school to end. So I could run over to Sean's place to bitch and moan about my father's announcement that morning.

"Crap, Sean, I'll need that hymen after all."

Sean spat out his rum and coke, trying to control his laughter.

"Not funny, Sean. I'm serious. My parents are making my wedding plans. They've already set a date. It's on the twenty-eighth of next month."

Sean couldn't speak. He doubled over, holding his stomach while continuing to laugh at my predicament.

"Dude, you suck. You are not helping whatsoever."

"Sorry, Fi. It's just too ridiculous."

"Exactly. It's ludicrous. Who the hell expects you to get married after an overnight crabbing trip?"

"Your dad." Sean burst out laughing again.

"He was serious!"

"I know. Have you talked to Don yet?"

"Oh God, no. I didn't even think about that. Do you think he's going along with this?"

"That's something that you are going to have to ask him, Fi."

"But I don't want to talk to Don ever again."

"It doesn't look like you have much of a choice."

Sean was right.

"Fi, why don't you just tell your dad no?"

Because I've already done that a million times. And it has never worked once. I also didn't want my father's silent treatment or the awkward tension in my house. And most importantly, I didn't want him blaming my mother for my impudence.

To remind me that I was still in America, the land of the free, the nation where you didn't have to marry the boy who took you on an overnight crabbing trip, Sean bought me fifteen dollar drinks at XYZ, a trendy, upscale South of Market bar. The watering hole for investment bankers, corporate lawyers, people who can afford to shell out over ten dollars for a drink.

"Look at these people, Fi. They think they are going to live forever."

"Stupid them."

I put my head down on my folded arms, feeling the effects of the Raging Bull and the events of the day.

"Buck up, Fi. The situation is not lost. Your Dad is not going to have you killed for not marrying Don. Not in this country anyway. And look on the bright side, no one lives forever."

"Well, I don't want to die any time soon."

"*You* don't have to. Where is this Don anyway?"

I knew what Sean was really asking, but I didn't want to tell him. The situation had not come to that point yet.

"Menlo Park somewhere," I lied.

Sean looked at me. I turned a shade of pink, feeling sure that he knew that I was lying. He always could tell when someone was lying, especially when that someone was me.

"No worries, Fi. I'm leaving Don completely to you. But just so you know, there is no shortage of roofies or peanuts."

"Good to know, Sean."

Peanuts.

The peanut, also known in the scientific community as *Arachis hypogaea*, is the most commonly-consumed nut in America. M&M's. Snickers. Nutrageous. PayDay. Planters. Peanuts are everywhere. They are a rich source of protein and niacin, which contribute to brain health, brain circulation and blood flow. Unless, of course, you are severely allergic to peanuts, in which case, they just contribute to your death.

Like Don.

Some people are more conducive to death. Others aren't. Shoot Rambo a dozen times and the guy keeps on going. Give Don a peanut and he'll just die on you. No good, unless you had a big life insurance policy on him. Or needed to get out of an arranged marriage to him.

A loud sigh from Sean interrupted my thoughts of peanuts. "Fi, I'm bored."

"My goodness, Sean, you have a front row seat at the meat market of the rich and famous. Take a look at all the silly people who think they're going to live forever, downing pricey drinks and waiting for someone to put them out of their misery."

Sean laughed. "Oh, Fi. You're the best."

"Yup. Like that sexy brunette at the end of bar. The one with the silvery, pink scarf hanging on her neck. She comes ready with death accessories. Aren't those the best ones?"

"You're learning, Fi. Always use something that belongs to them. You remember that." Sean winked at me.

"Oh I will." As Sean finished his drink, a question popped into my mind. "Why plastic surgery, Sean? Why make women prettier when…?"

"I was wondering when you were going to ask me that. I don't make people prettier. I do reconstruction, mostly. I fix whatever gets broken or destroyed. Like hymens." He laughed. "Gotta run. God's work waits for no one."

Sean made a beeline for the brunette. I downed the rest of my drink and headed home.

Reconstruction. Guess that explained that.

BEFORE GOING TO SLEEP, I emailed Don and told him to call me on Saturday. When he called me in the afternoon, I was still at home, too hung-over to drag myself into the office.

"Hi, Fiona. Aren't you excited about getting married?"

"No, Don. I'm not marrying you. We are not getting married."

"But it's already been arranged. Our parents agreed on it."

"Then unarrange it. Tell them to marry each other."

"Are you upset? You sound upset."

"Yes, Don. I'm upset. No one asked me about this. I don't agree to this. I'm not in love with you. And I'm not marrying you."

"Oh."

"You can tell your parents that for me. Marriage not happening."

"What does your dad say?"

"It doesn't matter, unless he's the one saying 'I do.' And he's not."

"Oh, so you don't want to get married?"

"No. Not to you." For the millionth time.

"But I just bought my own house here in San Bruno. It's a block away from my parents."

"Congratulations, Don. Good for you. Have a nice life in your house."

"It's a really nice house. To raise a family in."

"Good. Go raise a family in it. So long as it doesn't involve me."

"Fiona, why are you acting like this?"

"Like what?"

"Like you don't want to get married."

"Because I don't. I don't know how many times I have to say this, but I'm not going along with this. And nothing you can say will make me change my mind."

"Oh."

"Are we clear?"

"My Dad wants to talk to you."

Great.

Don handed the phone to his father.

"Hello? Fiona? This is Don's father."

"Hi, I'm not marrying Don."

"Didn't you have a nice time crabbing?"

"Not really. Cold and wet. And his friend died."

"But Don said you two had fun the whole night long."

"No, we didn't. Don fell asleep early on in the evening after he pulled up his crabs."

"But my son is a wonderful boy."

"I'm sure he is."

"He just bought his own house. Why don't you come over and see it? We're having a house-warming party next week."

"No, that's okay. I'm busy. Working. Lots of work."

"Just for a little while. It's a lovely house. You're going to love it."

"It doesn't matter. I'm not marrying Don."

"Fiona, can I speak with your father for a minute?"

Great.

I shook the receiver at to my father who had just come out of the bathroom. A pungent smell of human fecal matter followed him out into the hallway. I said nothing. People culture observed, even at home.

"Don's father, Dad. Tell him I'm not marrying Don. This is stupid."

"Fiona, don't be rude."

My father took the phone, holding his pajama bottoms up with his other hand as the elastic band had worn away.

"Hilo?"

I walked back into my bedroom to lie down and nurse my pounding headache. I had had one too many Raging Bulls last night. I muffled the sounds outside my room by hiding under the covers. I really didn't care what my father was saying to Don's father. I had already made my intentions clear.

"Wow, really? That's wonderful," I heard my father say. I pulled down the covers. Suddenly, I became interested in the conversation again.

"Of course, we'll be there. Don is such a good boy."

No, he isn't.

"I'll tell Fiona. She'll love it."

No, I won't, whatever "it" is.

"Okay. See you tomorrow."

My father padded into my room, still holding up his pajama bottoms.

"Guess what? Don's invited us to his house for dinner tomorrow night."

"Dad, I'm not going."

"Fiona, don't be rude."

"I'm not being rude. I'm being honest. I'm not going to marry the boy. There's no point in going to see his house or to eat dinner with his family."

"Well, I already said yes, so you have to come."

"No, Dad, you said yes. So you go."

"Fiona, it's just dinner."

"No, it's not. Don wants me to move in that house with him to be his cooking whore."

"Fiona! That's enough. There's no need to be vulgar. No harm in just having dinner, and we'll be there."

"I can't. I have to work."

"It's Sunday."

"Yeah, and I'm a big firm lawyer. Sunday is a working day."

"You will still need to eat. Might as well get a free meal at Don's place."

"No such thing as a free meal, Dad. I'm not going."

"We'll eat and leave."

"No, we won't. We're going to sit around and bullshit with them after dinner."

"No, I promise. We won't."

"And I'm not marrying Don."

"Well, then you'll get to tell him face to face tomorrow at dinner."

Like that was going to go down better.

"Fine, Dad."

"You'll go?"

"To tell Don and his family that I'm not marrying him."

A second later, I realized that I had been suckered into going on a third date with Don. And this time at his new house.

I needed more than a packet of roofies. I needed a Snickers bar.

CHAPTER
SIXTEEN

TRIAL LAWYERS SOMETIMES repeat the same question over and over, ignoring your response in an attempt to elicit the answer they want. It's an old cross-examination technique to try and wear down the witness. In court, judges and lawyers call it badgering. And the proper objection is "asked and answered." Because the question has already been asked and answered.

Move on, Counsel.

Unfortunately, the rules of California evidence do not apply to Chinese family dinners. Or to Chinese parents eager to marry off their offspring.

On Sunday evening, my parents picked me up at my office. They were afraid that I was going to sneak off somewhere, which was exactly what I had planned to do. Their surprise arrival foiled my escape plans. So I ended up in the family car headed for San Bruno with a Snickers bar in my purse.

Just in case.

"In and out. I'm not staying a minute longer, Dad."

"Don't be rude, Fiona."

Because Hello Kitty is never rude.

"Dad, I'm not being rude. I'm just telling you flat out what I've decided. I'm not marrying Don. And dinner is not going to change that."

"Just see his house first."

That actually works in Jane Austen's world. Lizzie Bennett doesn't realize how much she's in love with Mr. Darcy until she sees how grand Pemberly is. All of a sudden, she discovers how much she loves him when she sees the size of his estate. And not a moment before. Funny, love is. Even in Jane Austen's time.

But unlike Lizzie, I work for my living. I slave away for Jack Betner so I don't have to marry someone like Don to have three meals and a roof over my head. I probably make more money than Don. And estates here in America are not entailed.

God bless America. All of America, even San Bruno. Less power to the penis.

San Bruno is a Bay Area suburb with a population of about forty thousand. The city's highlights include San Francisco International Airport, Golden Gate National Cemetery, and thousands of one-and two-storied houses. Don had a two-story stucco home, in which the ground floor had been converted into a garage. So finding parking would never be an issue for the master and mistress of the house. But it was not Pemberly.

"What do you think, Fiona?" asked Don's father.

"It's a very nice house," I replied flatly.

"Wait until you see the inside."

Oh joy.

Home Depot and IKEA, not Ethan Allen, furnished the inside

of Don's new house. The resulting décor was American suburbia mixed with a touch of old Asia with an altar dedicated to Don's ancestors. Black and white photographs of his great-grandfather and grandfather stood in gilded frames on the mantle, accompanied by incense burners and plates of fruit. Plates of oranges, apples, bananas, pears. That's what the spirits of Chinese ancestors eat. And the smoke from the incense.

Bon appétit.

A set of free weights and a bench press sat in a corner of the living room. A weight bar leaned against the wall, looking out of place in the otherwise unremarkable space.

"Who lifts weights?" I asked.

"I do," replied Don.

I stared at his blubbery arms, arms that wiggled and jiggled like Jell-O when he moved them. If Don lifted weights, then I was a champion bodybuilder.

"Well, I'm just starting to," Don admitted sheepishly.

Really.

"I want to look good, you know, for stuff," he continued.

For our wedding.

I opened my mouth, ready to set Don straight again for the millionth time, but my father spoke first.

"Keeping fit is important, Don. You should encourage Fiona here to work out. All she does is sit in front of a computer all day. Not good for her. She needs to look good too," my father said.

"Dad, I look fine. And sitting in front of the computer is what I call working."

"You work too much."

"That's what lawyers do, Dad."

"I think it's so impressive that you are a lawyer," said Don.

"Uh, thanks."

"You should still be healthy, Fiona," my father insisted.

"Why? It's not like I have to look good in a wedding dress."

Oh darn. I went and kicked the proverbial pink elephant in the living room. And it farted. Loud.

Now everyone had to acknowledge it or suffocate in its fart.

"Fiona, look around. It's such a lovely house. You will be so happy here," my father said.

"No, I won't. Because I don't love Don here. Sorry, dude. Nothing personal."

"Uh, I need to go and check on the cornish hens," Don replied. He looked at his father and lowered his head.

"Fiona, don't be rude. Don is a good boy," reiterated my father.

"That's right. My boy will make a wonderful husband and father," Don's father said.

"Good. Marry him off to another girl. I don't want a husband, and I hate children. They just suck the life out of you. No thank you."

"Fiona, how can you say that? Children make a family," my mother said.

"My idea of a family is Pepito. Get used to it. He can be your grandson."

I hate children.

Even when I was one myself, I hated all the other kids. Children are always dirty, with sticky hands, runny noses, and ugly outfits. Children shit in their pants, pick their noses, eat their snot, and throw up their chocolate brownies. And they cry and whine for their mothers all the time. When I see children crying, I just want to shove logs of turd into their open mouths. That would teach them to shut up.

Or do what they do in Russian hospitals.

In the southern Ural town of Yekaterinburg, Russia, the hospital staff devised a simple, yet ingenious, way of dealing with crying infants. They gagged them, taping shut their screaming pie holes. Problem solved.

People started accusing the hospital of child abuse, even though the babies started it. Children get away with abuse all the time.

I already have Jack to abuse me. I don't need children.

"Don't be ridiculous, Fiona. Don, don't listen to her. She loves children," my father said quickly.

I ignored him.

"Pepito is great. When I get sick of him, I can just shove him into his cage with his seed and water tray. I can't exactly do that with children now, can I?"

"Who's Pepito?" asked Don's father.

"Nobody. It's her parakeet," my mother said.

"Oh."

"It doesn't matter. I'm still not marrying Don. I thought I should tell you all in person."

And I did. Don, his father, his mother, his grandmother, his aunt, and his little sister, who kept giving me sad looks. Probably because I was telling them all that I didn't want to live in that lovely house in San Bruno.

"But Don said you had a great time crabbing with him," said Don's father.

"I didn't. It sucked. It was cold, boring, and disgusting. And his friend died." No one seemed to remember that Carl drowned.

"But the crabs Don caught were delicious."

"I wouldn't know, sir. I didn't have any."

"Oh, Don cooked them for his mother. My boy can cook."

"Then you marry him."

"Fiona! Don't be rude," chastized my father.

"Oh no, it's okay. I understand now," said Don's father. "You're jealous because he didn't save the crabs for you."

"I hate crab. I didn't want to eat his stupid crabs."

"It's okay. He'll make you crab another time."

"No, it's not okay. You're not listening. I don't want to eat his crabs. I don't want to marry him!"

Asked and answered, asked and answered! Objection, your honor. Someone, anyone. I wanted to scream.

Don walked back into the living room and announced that dinner was ready. A full course Chinese dinner, family style, prepared by Don's father. Cornish hen, Chinese broccoli, beef stir fry, sauteed shrimp, vegetable medley, pan-roasted sea bass. And of course, steamed white rice. A meal is never a meal without steamed white rice.

"See what wonderful things Don can cook? Isn't Don great?" said Don's mother.

"Don, did you cook all this by yourself?" I asked.

"Well, my dad helped me a little."

While you were probably busy eating in the kitchen. A little, my ass.

I stuffed my mouth with Chinese broccoli before I spat out anything rude, keeping my eyes on my bowl. I started counting the grains of rice I picked up with my chopsticks, trying to remain civil like a good Hello Kitty.

"Fiona can't cook at all," said my father.

"I'm sure she can learn," said Don's mother.

"No, I hate cooking. About as much as I hate children."

"I didn't know how to cook when I married Don's father. But I learned. You just have to be willing to learn. Eating out all the time is very expensive and unhealthy."

I said nothing and continued eating.

"Your dad says you help out at the laundromat, right?" continued Don's mother. "That's wonderful. You know how to do laundry."

"I take the tickets and work the cash register while I chit-chat with the customers. I don't do laundry."

I break up marriages, sow discord, and amuse myself with the pain and anguish of fighting couples, lady.

"Don't worry. Don has a really nice washer and dryer in the basement. You won't have to lug clothes to the laudromat."

I looked at Don who was busy peeling apart his cornish hen. I wanted to reach over and smack his doughy, fat face. To tear the cornish hen from his fingers and bash his head with it. So that he would say something, anything.

But Don just munched away, licking his greasy fingers. He kept his head down to avoid any eye contact with me, confirming all my fears. He was not going to stand up to his parents. Nutless twit. Either that or he too was trapped. Perhaps he too did not want to be ostracized for disobeying his parents. Maybe we weren't that different after all.

"This house is perfect for starting a family," said Don's mother.

I said nothing and chewed my vegetables. I thought about

the Snickers in my purse, wondering if it had melted.

"The schools here are great and it's a pretty safe neighborhood," she continued.

"Who cares? I'm done with school."

"For the children, Fiona."

"I'm not having kids. Not with Don."

"Children are wonderful. They make the family."

"No they are not. They ruin your life."

They eat you out of Dior shoes and Gucci handbags. Then they grow up and have more leeches and parasites of their own which they'll dump on you any given night with no notice so they can make more of those creatures. And spend their time shopping at Target and eating at Applebee's. Unless, of course, they turn out to be the next Ted Bundy or Jack Unteweger, ridding society of excess women. Then people will just throw eggs at your door and blame you for birthing the little monster.

No thank you.

"Fiona doesn't mean that," said my father. He laughed nervously and said, "Don't listen to her. She says no when she means yes."

The classic defense of rapists.

I rolled my eyes, tired of repeating the same things over and over again. When no one bothered to listen at all. Not even once.

As soon as dinner ended, I stood up, impatient to leave. My parents pretended not to notice me stamping my foot on Don's beige carpet.

"Did you like your dinner, Fiona?" Don's father asked.

"Yes, it was delicious. Thank you." It was.

"See, Don is wonderful, isn't he?"

Not again.

"I'm sure you think so, sir. Thanks for dinner, but I really have to get back to work now."

"Okay, I'll let you two say goodnight alone." Don's father winked at me, and his mother started giggling. They stepped onto the front porch with my parents, leaving me alone with Don.

Fiona and Don, sitting in a tree, k-i-s-s-i-n-g.

"Good night, Don. Thanks for dinner. You're very nice. But I'm not marrying you. I'm sure you'll find someone more suitable."

There, I had said it as clearly and directly as I could. There could be no more further misunderstandings or miscommunications.

He nodded and smiled. "So you want to come over next Saturday?"

"What?"

"Next Saturday. For dinner again."

"No. No dinner. Not next Saturday. Not ever. Good-bye, Don."

Without waiting for him to respond, I marched out the front door and got into the back of my parents' car.

"Let's go home."

"Did you guys kiss?" asked my mother.

"No. I told him I wasn't going to see him anymore. No dinners. No wedding. No kiss."

And that was that.

CHAPTER
SEVENTEEN

"IT'S NOT SO MUCH ABOUT standing up for yourself, Fi. It's about giving them what they're asking for. 'You just need the will to do what the other guy wouldn't,'" said Sean, quoting Keyser Söze. *The Usual Suspects* was Sean's favorite movie, followed by *American Psycho* and *A Clockwork Orange*.

Sean always knew how to deal with bullies, on and off the playground. Again, thanks to his old man. Give them what they're asking for. Like how he gave Stephanie what she asked for.

And Evan, who all the kids in Sean's old neighborhood had dubbed Evan the Terrible, learned what Keyser meant. Courtesy of Sean himself.

Two heads taller than any kid on the block, Evan rained terror on every child with a little help from Buddy, his oversized German Shepherd. His parents, too busy working when they weren't partaking in some good old-fashioned domestic violence, ignored their son's foibles. Evan patrolled the neighborhood, taking lunch money, giving wedgies, thumping heads against

curb while Buddy chased the bloodied victim up a tree, over
fence, or worse.

Sean became Evan's favorite target. So he decided that Evan
and Buddy had to go. He waited for them on his front porch every
day after school, accompanied by a spray bottle filled with lighter
fluid, his Zippo, and his father's baseball bat.

"Home court advantage," Sean told me afterwards.

One day, Sean got his wish. Within fifteen minutes, the stench
of burnt dog filled the air while Evan lay on the ground with a
broken collar bone and a cracked skull. Sean retrieved Buddy's
scorched dog tags and gave them to me after we became friends.
After I thumped Jeremy good and proper.

"Remember, Fi. No fear. Just do what the other guy would
never do."

Sean did what Evan could never do.

The problem is that bullies grow up. They leave the playground, school, and neighborhood, and become attending phy-
sicians, senior partners, vice presidents, and general managers.
Instead of giving you pink belly or thumping your lunch, they
force you to work overtime, change your schedule around, call
you incompetent, threaten to fire you, put you down in front of
your colleagues, impose impossible deadlines and wait for you
to fail. They become people you can't set on fire or pummel with
a crow bar.

And you become too old for juvie.

But they are still bullies. And you still have to deal with them.
Or they'll step on you every chance they get, even if you have
alphabet soup after your name.

Like Sean, I hated bullies.

"I need everything reviewed by the close of business, Fiona. Don't give me this shit about not enough time," Jack yelled with his office door wide open.

"Jack, there are five boxes of this stuff. The documents didn't come in until noon today."

"That's five hours, Fiona. Christ, my wife gave birth in less than that time. An hour a box."

"Jack, there are thousands of pages here. No way could I do all this myself. Why can't I split the piles with another associate?"

"Because we want consistent review."

Bullshit.

We were conducting due diligence for a major merger. Jack wanted me to review the entire set of documents delivered by the other side, catalog and summarize each one in a neat chart all by five o'clock the same day. All by myself. Thousands of agreements, leases, financial records, licenses, employment contracts.

"Laziness and incompetence are not tolerated here at Beamer & Hodgins. You should have this done in a snap. I can't believe you went to Yale."

Yale.

My albatross. People who didn't go to an Ivy League college will take every opportunity to put you down, to prove to themselves they are smarter and better than you. That the Ivies aren't all that and neither are you.

So when you don't walk on water, read minds, predict the financial future, or finish twenty-hour projects in five, you are incompetent, stupid, lazy, less than them, proving that the best and the brightest didn't go to Yale, Harvard, or Princeton. They went to UCLA or Cal, like Jack did.

Jack tossed my half-finished chart back at me.

"Get this crap out of my face, and bring me some hot decaf coffee. Sugar, no cream. I need to take my heart pills."

Jack had heart problems. His heart didn't contract properly, so to keep it working effectively, he took digoxin, a form of digitalis. He pulled out his vial and popped off the cap with too much force. The pills tumbled out onto his desk and floor.

"Fucking son of a bitch. Look at what you made me do. Go! Now!" he screamed when I stooped down, trying to help him pick up the pills.

So I left with my inadequate analysis chart and four tablets of digoxin. I went into the break room and got Jack his hot decaf sweetened with sugar and no cream. And digoxin. Crushed, dissolved, and stirred to smooth perfection.

"Here you go, Jack."

Talk about using something from the victim.

Because I couldn't set him on fire or beat him with a tire iron. But Jack had asked for it. For Fiona thumping.

I went back to my office, wondering where I had put Buddy's tags from all those years ago.

I studied the painted portrait of a long-faced lady with her hair pulled back that I had put up on my desktop. Instead of Ted Bundy, I had chosen Marie Delphine Macarty, or Delphine LaLaurie, or as history would know her, Madame LaLaurie.

The Paris Hilton of New Orleans in the early 1830's, Delphine threw lavish parties for the elite who adored her until they found out she had been playing plastic surgeon with her slaves in her attic. She gave one a sex change, turned one into a human crab, and another into a caterpillar by slicing, dicing, and resetting limbs with the help of her surgeon husband. She even chained one woman up with her own intestines. She definitely used things belonging to the victim. So they ran her out of town.

"Who's that?" my new secretary asked when I first put Delphine's picture up.

"A true role model for women."

Girl power.

Suddenly, someone screamed out in the hall, silencing clacking keyboards, mice, and water cooler chatter. Someone else began yelling for an ambulance. Someone gasped. Someone started running around outside. Everyone at Beamer & Hodgins sprang to life with noise and movement, everyone except Jack.

WITH AN INDEFINITE extension for my due diligence project, I took the afternoon off and went home.

"Why are you home early?" my mother asked. "You didn't get fired, did you?"

"No. I took the afternoon off."

"Why?"

"Boss suffered heart failure. Bad vibes at the firm."

"Oh, that's terrible. But it's good that you are home. Your father has something to tell you."

My father shuffled out to the dining room where my mother was sweeping up the crumbs he had left behind from his lunch.

"You're home early. You didn't get fired, did you?"

"No. Mom just asked me that."

"Oh. Okay. Well, I have some good news."

"What?"

"We've booked your wedding reception at the Empress Restaurant. So lucky that weekend was free."

"What wedding reception? I told you I'm not marrying Don."

"Then why did you agree to have dinner with Don and his family?"

"Oh my God! Dad, you are unbelievable! I went because you dragged me. I went to tell them explicitly to their faces that I wasn't going to marry Don! What the hell is wrong with you people?"

"But didn't you guys talk and kiss when you left?"

"No! No! No! We didn't. I told him I never wanted to see him again."

"Well, we already booked the place."

"Then unbook it! Unless you want to marry Don."

"Fiona, stop shouting."

"Then stop trying to marry me off to Don. He's a total loser."

I marched out of the house, slamming the door behind me. Anger blinded me, propelling my legs one in front of the other. I had no idea where I was headed, only that I was headed away from my house, away from any talk of marrying Don. I walked until my legs were tired and the sun began to set. And I found myself once again at Sean's place on Russian Hill.

But Sean wasn't home.

"Dr. Killroy is with a patient," said his receptionist when I called him at his office. "May I take a message?"

No, you may not.

Bullies come in all shapes, sizes, forms. Jeremy, Stephanie, Evan, Buddy, Jack, my father, Don. And I needed to deal with them on my own. Like Sean did, without fear, without remorse. Because they were asking for it. Because I was tired of taking it.

"Don?"

"Fiona?"

"Yeah, hey, your offer for dinner on Saturday still good?"

"Uh, sure. My dad said you would change your mind."

"Really? Guess he was right. But listen, let's have dinner just the two of us. At your place."

"Oh, okay. I'll make crab."

"You do that."

A weight lifted from my chest, along with all the anger and frustration. Making up my mind and settling on a solution to my problem changed my mood from helpless to hopeful. It gave new energy to my tired legs, powering my walk home.

By the time I returned, my mother had dinner on the table. One of the benefits of living at home. My mother made sirloin steak with steamed rice and vegetables. My favorite.

"Fiona, where did you go?"

"Oh, nowhere, Mom. I just went for a walk."

"Your father and I were worried about you."

"Oh, I'm fine. I'm having dinner with Don this Saturday."

My mother looked at me, surprised.

"I thought you said you weren't going to see him again."

"Well, I changed my mind. I think I need to sort things out with him."

"Oh good, your father will be so pleased."

"But I'm having dinner alone with him at his house."

"Alone? The two of you?"

"Yes. We shared a tent already, remember? Out in the middle

of nowhere under the stars. Dinner in San Bruno can hardly top that."

"Fiona, don't be facetious. I guess it's a good idea for you two young people to talk by yourselves."

"Yes, Mom. Talking is good."

After dinner, I retreated to the quiet of my room and reveled in my thoughts. Thoughts of Don, thoughts of peanuts, thoughts of Don and peanuts. I paced back and forth in the dark with my iPod with Cobain crooning in my ears.

I've been locked inside your heart shaped box, for weeks

Insanity.

It's part of being Chinese-American, having to deal with insanity. Whether you are driven to it by your parents, by your peers, by expectations, by nonsensical logic, by cultural superstitions, it doesn't matter. Eventually, you end up in the same place and find yourself thinking about engaging Snickers or PayDays in unintended uses.

Like I did with Lidocaine and Mr. Happy.

I've been drawn into your magnet tar pit trap

Don. Like a deadly cancer, he was metastasizing through my life slowly, insiduously, relentlessly. You can't ignore cancer away or walk away from it or tell it off. Cancer must be physically eliminated, cut out and chucked into a biohazard bag. And burned in a high degree furnace.

I wish I could eat your cancer when you turn black

I barely heard my cell phone ring with my headphones on, but I picked up when it vibrated itself off my desk onto the floor. It was Sean.

I pulled out my left earpiece.

"Hey, what's up, Fi?"

"Oh hey, you won't believe what happened at work today."

I started to tell Sean about Jack and the digoxin.

"Fi, okay, stop right there. First rule of doing God's work: You never talk about doing God's work. To anyone, Fi. You hear me? No one." *Fight Club*, another one of Sean's favorite movies.

"But…"

"No buts. You never know who is going to sell you out."

"But, you…"

"No, Fi. Suspecting something is one thing. Talking about it explicitly is quite another. Not even to me, you hear?"

"I hear."

"Self-preservation, Fi. We're too old to go to juvie. And you never know if someone is taping the conversation."

Forever in debt to your priceless advice

"Got it."

"Good girl. Now tell me, what are you doing this weekend?"

"Second rule of doing God's work, Sean. Never ask one question too many. I have something to take care of this weekend."

Sean laughed.

"Good girl, Fi. Now you're learning. Need any roofies?"

"No, I'm good with Snickers."

Sean chuckled.

"Fi?"

"Yeah, Sean?"

"It's about time."

CHAPTER
EIGHTEEN

POISONING IS ALWAYS CONSIDERED first degree murder because it shows that you took time to pick out a poison, procure it, and use it on your victim. You thought and planned and had time to decide otherwise. Prosecutors call that premeditation.

And you get twenty-five to life for murder one.

You get less time if you jump out of your car and use a tire iron to bash in the skull of the person who cut you off on the highway. There wasn't time to cool down and regain your good senses. You were too pissed off to realize what you were doing. Spur of the moment killing gets you murder two.

And you can also blame it on road rage or some twisted sense of self-defense. You thought he or she was trying to get you.

But the safest way to do God's work is to make things look like an accident. A fall down the stairs, a slip in the tub, a faulty garage door. Make it look like God is doing His own work.

Accidental overdose with chemical substances works too, so long as it's not arsenic, strychnine, or the now-popular succinocholine. Those chemicals scream murder thanks to overuse in literature and real life. And nobody gets up and takes their regular two tablets of arsenic in the morning. It just doesn't have any health benefits.

Unlike digoxin. People take digoxin to stay alive. And sometimes, they accidentally take a little too much. In Jack's case, too much of a good thing was anything but wonderful.

"Oh my God, I can't believe he's gone," sobbed Margot, Jack's faithful old-school secretary. In her mid-fifties, she wore blouses that tied into a bow at the neck and skirts with the hem right below the knee. She pulled her graying hair back into a low bun. With her tortoise-shell framed glasses, she looked like a secretary out of the movies.

"What happened?" I asked.

"He must have taken too many of his heart pills again." Margot blew her nose into a Kleenex.

"Again?"

"He did that once before, a couple of years ago. We almost lost him then."

Poor Jack.

So Jack had a history of being careless with his heart medication. And Margot, being an ultra-efficient secretary, had washed the coffee cup and cleaned up his office to await his return. God bless Margot.

I breathed a sigh of relief.

Killers don't really think about getting caught and having to face the consequences when they decide to do God's work. If they did, no one would ever do it. Death Row would be empty. It's like flying. You can't get in that cockpit if you are terrified of falling out of the sky. You just have to believe that if you do everything right, the laws of physics and aerodynamics will keep you in the air.

I believed that the laws of karma would keep me out of jail. Jack had it coming.

"You'll be working for me now, Fiona," said Doreen, another senior partner in the corporate and securities department.

Another Jack, only in a skirt. Same shit, different partner.

"The merger has to go according to schedule. I need that due diligence report by tomorrow."

Yes, Doreen.

Anything you say, Doreen. So long as you ask civilly.

SEAN WANTED TO STAY in and watch the *Law & Order: Criminal Intent* marathon on T.V. on Friday evening. And I needed some company after my somewhat traumatic week.

"At least you still have your job, Fi," he told me.

"Yeah, I thought they were going to lay me off with Jack gone."

"Nah, trust me. Doreen should be more than happy to swoop down and take over Jack's clients."

"Oh my God, Sean, that's exactly what she did as soon as we got the news that Jack wasn't coming back."

"How ruthlessly corporate. So you looking forward to tomorrow's dinner with your fiance?"

"Yup. I have a surprise for Don, and I can't wait to give it to him."

Sean munched on a Ruffles sour cream & cheddar chip, mulling over his thoughts. For a full minute, he didn't say anything.

"Fi, be careful. If the opportunity doesn't present itself, let it go."

"I know."

"Seriously. It's all about timing and opportunity."

"I know."

"I would hate to lose my sailing buddy, Fi." Sean continued to crunch, washing down his Ruffles with beer. "Where does this guy work?"

"Forget it, Sean."

"Okay, but seriously, be careful. Whatever happens, don't panic. Fear and panic make you stupid. Don't be stupid."

"I know."

"And it makes you look suspicious."

"I know."

"Opportunity and timing. Remember that."

"I will."

Sean always looked out for me, ever since that time he inspired me to thump Jeremy in the schoolyard.

ON SATURDAY EVENING, I drove down to San Bruno to have dinner with Don, snacking on Snickers bars. Snickers really is the best candy bar ever produced, consisting of peanut butter nougat topped with roasted peanuts and caramel covered with milk chocolate. According to Wikipedia, it's the "best selling chocolate bar of all time and has annual global sales of U.S. $2 billion."

But the peanut butter nougat and caramel make finely-chewed bits of peanut stick to your teeth, gums, tongue, and lips, making it extremely dangerous to kiss someone who has a severe peanut allergy. Accidental poisoning with peanuts.

"But Officer, *I* ate the Snickers. Not Don."

"Did you know that he was allergic to peanuts?"

"Yes. That's why I didn't offer him one."

Oops. Hello Kitty forgot to rinse her mouth out with Listerine before kissing her boyfriend.

I parked my car and threw away the Snickers wrappers in a public trash bin. I didn't want anyone to find five empty wrappers in my car. Eating that many Snickers before going over to Don's place for a crab dinner would look suspicious.

I strode up the block in a floral dress and my four-inch Prada stilettos, pounding on the pavement hard. The pain shooting up my calves strengthened my resolve to do God's work properly, efficiently, the way it should be done.

Don greeted me wearing workout clothes. Tank top and shorts. His fat arms wiggled, brushing against his body as he walked. His belly hung over the elastic top of his shorts. The hazards of being the son of a chef.

"The crabs are cooking."

"That's great, Don. Can't wait for dinner."

"I was going to work out a little before dinner. You wanna watch?"

"Sure."

What an exciting treat before dinner. Getting to watch Don lift weights. I felt like one of those girls who got to watch her boyfriend at football practice in high school. One of the girls in the "in" crowd.

"I think I can bench press one-eighty, Fiona."

"Really?"

"Yeah. Wanna spot me?"

"Sure."

Like I would really save him if he lost his grip and the bar fell on his throat.

Don lay down on the bench and gripped the weight bar, struggling a little to shift his bulky form under the bar on the slender bench.

"Can you slide on two more ten-pound weights?"

Sure.

And there it was. Opportunity presented itself, along with perfect timing, as Don adjusted his hold on the bar.

I bypassed the ten-pound weights Don had requested, and quickly slipped a twenty-pound disk on each side of the bar.

"Okay. You're good to go, honey."

And where you're going, there's no coming back.

Don gritted his teeth and hefted the bar off its holder. All two hundred pounds of it. His arms shook as he brought the weight towards his chest and pushed it back up. His face, red with exertion, broke out in sweat.

One.

"You doing okay, Don?"

"Ya…"

Two.

Don's cheeks, now the color of beets, puffed in and out as he struggled to push the two hundred pounds up. But he didn't set the weights down. I had to hand it to him. Don was dying to try and impress me. Literally.

Three.

Four.

Five.

Then it happened.

Don lost his grip and the bar crashed down on his chest, rolling onto his throat. He gagged as the two hundred pounds crushed against his windpipe. And his arms, too tired from lifting, flailed helplessly as he tried to pry the bar off himself.

"Help…"

If your husband, wife, child, mother, or father is drowning and you do nothing, you're liable for their death. Because you have a duty to rescue them, or at least try, by virtue of your relationship to them. So says black letter law.

But that obligation doesn't apply to bystanders, strangers, friends, acquaintances, or the boy that your father is trying to force you to marry. You have no duty to save a stranger, unless you start saving them. Then you have to continue with your rescue. Because your efforts will make everyone else think they don't need to help.

Just ask the thirty-eight people who watched Kitty Genovese get stabbed to death and did nothing. Not one of her neighbors was held liable.

"The bar is too heavy for me, Don. I'm going to call 911."

I didn't even have to kiss him. All I had to do was nothing, for about five minutes.

Don's face turned purple. He made a curious gurgling sound in his throat as he struggled to breathe. But the bar pressed down heavy and tight until his eyes looked up at me, glassy, lifeless.

"Emergency? I need help. My friend just had an accident with his weights. Please send an ambulance. Quick."

And it was an accident. Kind of.

The paramedics came and wheeled Don off to the hospital, but it was already too late. His brain had been deprived of oxygen for too long.

Thank God I ate all those Snickers bars. I didn't get home until midnight. As soon as I opened the door, my father accosted me with questions.

"Why are you home so late? How was your dinner?"

"Don died."

"What? What do you mean?"

"Don died. Don is dead."

"How? What happened?"

"He was lifting weights, trying to impress me. He slipped and the bar crushed his throat."

"Fiona, this is not funny. Tell me the truth."

"That is the truth. Don is dead."

"Did you call an ambulance? Did you try to help him?"

"Of course I called an ambulance. But it was too late."

"Oh my God," wailed my mother. She too had been waiting up for me. "What about his parents?"

"The hospital called them, Mom."

"Did you have dinner, Fiona?"

"No, I'm kind of hungry, actually."

"You poor thing. It's not your fault. I'll make you some ramen noodles."

Ramen noodles. Chinese comfort food. I love my mother.

She is the best. Always ready with a soothing word and a pack of ramen noodles and chicken broth.

I SLEPT WONDERFULLY that night and got up early. Instead of being full of energy, I woke up constipated, thanks to all the Snickers bars. Damn Don. It was all his fault I had to spend Saturday morning on the toilet before heading to work. That boy was nothing but trouble.

When I arrived at my office, I went online and found the following news article:

> **San Bruno Man Crushed to Death:** Don Koo, 30, of San Bruno, died yesterday evening at his home when he unsuccessfully tried to bench press 200 pounds. The bar slipped and crashed down on his throat, crushing his windpipe. Koo's fiancée, Fiona Yu, an attorney at the prestigious San Francisco law firm of Beamer & Hodgins LLP, called emergency services but paramedics were unable to revive Koo despite repeated attempts.

The article continued to discuss the importance of safety measures while exercising and lifting weights, including the use of a strong and able spotter. The usual trite discussion. Then I suddenly remembered I never even talked to a reporter. Maybe the nutters who think the government is invading their brain with radio waves were right. Maybe I needed to invest in an aluminum foil hat. Maybe not. Maybe they got it from the police or hospital report.

I stopped reading, picked up the phone and called Sean.

"Yeah?" answered a sleepy voice.

"It's me. Have you read the news?"

"No. I haven't even had my coffee yet, Fi. This better be good, darling."

"It's pretty good. I made the front page."

"You what?"

"Made the front page. Go online. Type in Don Koo. K-O-O."

"Oh God. Tell me you're not in jail."

"Sean, I'm not in jail. I'm at my office, working. Don't worry. God did His own work."

"Really?"

"Yeah, really. Just Google Don Koo."

"Okay, when I wake up."

"Go back to sleep, Sean."

"Fi?"

"Yeah?"

"I'm proud of you."

"Like you said, everyone has to die."

CHAPTER
NINETEEN

I LOVE FUNERALS. THEY are chock full of good energy, which is perfect for anyone who has a porous psyche. It's like bathing in pure sunlight.

I have a very porous psyche.

If you hated the decedent, you're glad—happy, even—that he's dead. If you loved the decedent, you're sad. You miss him and you grieve because you loved him. Either way, the resulting emotions come out positive. Good energy all around. No jealousy, envy, or spite like you would encounter at weddings.

Just pure love and perhaps a negligible dose of schadenfreude.

No one ever says, "I've been a pallbearer twenty-seven times and never the decedent. When do I get to be the one carried down the aisle?"

No one ever says, "I wish I was the one in the box with the pasty mortician makeup and the scent of formaldehyde."

And the nosy-parkers keep their mouths shut because no one ever asks, "So when do you plan to pop off? What kind of casket would you like? Mahogany or ebony?"

Most importantly, the decedent isn't running around stressed out, screaming at friends and family to make sure his big day goes exactly the way he's been dreaming about since the age of six. Because he can't. He's dead. He doesn't give a crap whether everyone has their nails done right or has their hair in place.

Best of all, you get to pig out at the wake without worrying about what everyone thinks. You're just drowning your sorrows in food.

I came home from Jack's funeral rosy-cheeked with a stomach full of homemade meatloaf, potato salad, and key lime pie.

But Chinese funerals ruin all that for me.

The numerous superstitions sap all the fun out. They are enough to scare someone to death. That's because improper funeral arrangements can bring bad luck and disaster on the decedent's family and anyone else who attends the funeral.

"Remember to light some incense and bow deeply, Fiona," said my father.

"When we get to the grave and the coffin is removed from the hearse and lowered into the ground, you must turn away," warned my mother.

Or you will die.

Or someone in your family will die.

Do anything improper and bad luck will follow you. So will Death.

And you will die.

It's dangerous business to attend a Chinese funeral.

"Don't wear that nice suit, Fiona," whispered my mother.

"Why? It's black."

"Because after the funeral, we'll have to burn it."

"What?"

"To avoid bad luck associated with death. Here, I bought you a cheap black suit from Ross."

My mother handed me a brand new, ninety-dollar Tahari suit. A discounted black suit to be worn once and burned. All because of Don.

"And remember, Fiona, we have to stop off at Safeway before we come home."

Because you don't want Death following you home. You go to Safeway or Albertsons to confuse Death, to lose him at the supermarket in the cereal aisle, hoping that he will be too distracted by the Club Card special and the selection of Grape Nuts, Cheerios, and Special K.

"Dad, are you sure we should be going to Don's funeral?"

"We have to. You were his fiancée."

Right.

"Don't you think his family might be a little mad at me?"

"For what? It was an accident. You tried to save him."

Right.

When we arrived at the funeral home, the greeter shouted, "Guests have arrived."

Don's family was seated next to the coffin. They looked up. Traditionally, they should have worn white tunics and sackcloth headdresses as a sign of mourning. Instead, the family decided to go with the American part of Chinese-America and wore black suits and dresses.

"First bow," said the greeter.

We bowed. Then we walked up towards the coffin.

"Second bow."

We bowed.

I lit some incense and raised it up to my forehead before placing it in the holder in front of the altar.

"Third bow."

We bowed.

"Family members thank the guests."

Don's family bowed to us in thanks. For braving Death itself by coming to Don's funeral. We bowed back.

Everyone sat in silence after that. Don's parents couldn't offer prayers to their son. According to Chinese custom, an elder should never show respect to someone younger. So if you die young, unmarried, and childless, too bad. No prayers for you.

It's even worse for dead babies. No funeral rites at all. Dead babies get tossed in the ground in silence because everyone's their elder.

Don was lucky he was getting a proper funeral at all.

"Don't we have to wear some kind of cloth or something?" I asked my father afterward, when we were standing in the dairy aisle at Safeway.

"No. Because he didn't have any children."

According to custom, the period of mourning by Don's family must continue for another hundred days, signified by wearing a piece of colored cloth on the sleeve of each of the family members. Black is worn by the deceased's children, blue by the grandchildren and green by the great-grandchildren. But Don didn't have any children. So no one had to wear anything.

But a period of mourning is not required if the deceased is a child or a wife. No need to mourn anyone you can replace easily.

"Oh, Fiona, I almost forgot. Out of respect for Don, you cannot date for at least a year."

"What?"

"You were his fiancée. That's almost like a wife. So you can't go on dates for a year."

"A year?"

"A year."

Hai, Daddy.

Because I would bring the shadow of death to other boys. It had nothing to do with respect for Don. But either way, I would be prearranged-date-free for a year. That's the upside of Chinese funerals. If you do everything right and obey all the rules, good luck follows you.

It really does.

I WALKED INTO MY OFFICE on Monday morning to find that all my files and books had disappeared. When I logged into my email, I noticed a new message from Human Resources.

> *Hi Fiona,*
>
> *Doreen has asked us to move you closer to her for her convenience. We've moved all your files and books to office C3. That's on the floor above yours. It's the one on Doreen's right. IT will be taking care of the phone and computer. No worries.*
>
> *Any questions, please let me know, okay?*
>
> *-Colleen, HR Manager*

For Doreen's convenience.

I went up to my new office, not knowing what to expect, but feeling relieved that I had not been laid off.

"Do you like it?"

I turned around to face Doreen.

"Yes, it's beautiful. It's so big."

"I hope you're not complaining that it's too big."

"No. No. This is great."

It was. The office was much bigger than Keener's office. It had a better view, being one floor higher. And a couch. A couch where I could read, put my tired, aching feet up after hours, and take a nap when I had to pull an all-nighter.

"Good, I'm glad you like it. You'll be spending tonight here. I need these three agreements by tomorrow morning." Doreen handed me three thick files and returned to her office.

"Sure."

Anything you say, Doreen.

I settled into my new office, burying my head in Doreen's contracts. I didn't even have time to put up a new desktop picture. Countess Elizabeth Bathory would just have to wait.

Around ten-thirty at night, my cell phone rang, pulling me out of an agreement-induced trance.

"Fi, it's me."

"Hey, Sean. What's up?"

"Can you come over tonight?"

"No can do, Sean. I got a new office. Right next to Doreen's and she's making me earn my keep. Why? What's up?"

"You think you can come over tomorrow?"

"Uh, I don't know. Is everything okay?"

"Can you at least take a break and swing by my place tomorrow evening? Please."

"Sure. What's this about?"

"I'll tell you when you get here."

"Sean?"

"Yeah, Fi?"

"Everything okay?"

"No."

"What's wrong?"

"You know what they say about luck, that it eventually runs out?"

"Yeah."

"Well, that's my problem. What time can you be here?"

"Like I said, I don't know. How about six, six-thirty?"

"Thanks. See you then."

The short conversation with Sean disturbed me, disrupting my concentration for the rest of the night. I had never known Sean to be worried, to lose his cool, to be anything but calm and totally under control.

Maybe Sean was losing it. Maybe his luck was indeed running out. Whatever it was, it had to be serious. His fear and unease stunk like human shit, like the time he crapped his tightie-whities when his father came and got him at school.

Sister Maria had caught Sean smoking behind his usual corner of the schoolyard. Except this time, Sean couldn't lie and say that the stamped-out cigarette butts on the ground belonged to someone else. He had a cigarette between his lips when Sister Maria spun him around by the shoulder.

"Class, Sean has something to tell everyone."

"No, I don't."

"Yes, you do. Tell everyone what I just caught you doing."

"Jerking off."

Our class burst out laughing. Sister Maria threatened us back into silence with detention slips.

"Sean, if you don't tell everyone what you were just doing, you'll be getting two weeks of detention instead of one."

"Okay, Sister. Everyone, I was smoking. Yes, smoking."

"And what did we learn about smoking, Sean?"

"That it's bad. That we'll go to hell for it."

"And why is smoking bad?"

"Because it gives us lung cancer. And because getting lung cancer hurts Jesus."

"That's right. Now, go to the principal's office."

I pretended I needed to use the restroom so that I could get out of class. I found Sean sitting on the bench outside Sister Carmen's office, where I had sat after thumping Jeremy.

Sean was pale. He rubbed the back of his neck. "Sister Carmen called my father. He's going to come and get me," he said.

"Well, at least you get to go home early."

"My father is going to kill me for stealing his cigarettes."

"No, he's not, Sean. He's probably just going to ground you or make you clean up your room."

"You don't know my father, Fi. He's going to beat the crap out of me."

When his father arrived, Sean got up and I smelled shit emanating from his seat. But like a true friend, I pretended not to notice that he had messed his undies. Even back then, I understood people culture.

And I knew he was right about the beating awaiting him at

home. No one craps his pants about suspended television and phone privileges.

Sean missed the next two days of school. Sister Maria marked him down as sick. When he returned to class, he had a note from his father which he showed me before giving it to Sister Maria.

> *Dear Sister,*
>
> *Sean was sick for the last two days. My son had severe stomach pains, gas, and uncontrollable diarrhea. Please excuse him.*
>
> *-Frank Deacon*

Adding insult to injury. Frank was an asshole.

But Sean hadn't asked me to come over the next day because he was afraid of getting another beating from his father—Frank was dead.

It sounded like Sean needed a major dose of good luck. He should have attended Don's funeral with me.

CHAPTER
TWENTY

E VERYONE KNOWS THAT THE best lie is a half-truth. Because a
lie flavored with a kernel of truth makes the lie taste more
like the real thing.

So long as the person you're lying to never finds out which
half is which.

Unfortunately, sometimes you're the person being told the
half-truth, and you're left wondering which half is which.

I buzzed Sean's apartment around six in the evening the
next day, itching with curiosity and excitement. From his sense
of urgency over the phone, I expected Sean to answer the door
immediately.

But he didn't.

I buzzed him again, keeping my thumb on the little white
button long enough to be rude.

No answer.

I called Sean on his cell phone. After a couple of rings, he
finally picked up. "Hey Sean, I half expected you to greet me in

your feather boa. But I think I'd settle for you just to buzz me in."

"Are you at my apartment, Fi?"

"Yes. You asked me to drop by last night, remember?"

"Oh, yeah. I remember. Listen, Fi, I'm a little busy at the moment. Can we meet up tomorrow instead?"

I heard seagulls crying in the background and suspected Sean was somewhere near the wharf or harbor.

"Sean, where are you?"

Sean ignored my question, which I took as a sign not to ask any further about his current whereabouts. To drive the point home, he changed the topic.

"How did Don's funeral go?"

"Not as lovely as Jack's. Holy Christ, you should have seen how much food people brought."

"People always bring too much food to wakes. Keeping their eyes on the cherry pie makes them feel less awkward."

"Like me." I laughed. "And it was key lime pie."

"So when are you going on your next date?"

"Not for another year, courtesy of Don's tragic and untimely demise."

"Oh?"

"Yeah, my father said custom is for the fiancée to mourn for a year. So no dating for me for 365 days."

"The fiancee. That's spectacular, Fi."

"Sean, is everything okay?"

"I need to take care of some things. I'll call you later." Sean hung up. He didn't even apologize for standing me up.

Part of me wanted to pry into whatever Sean was keeping back. Part of me wanted to utter the three magic words that allowed lawyers to be nosey-parkers and knowledge keepers without having to sleep with the fish.

"Attorney-client privilege. Anything you want to tell me, Sean?"

But I knew Sean too well. He would not have appreciated any insinuation that he needed to speak within the privilege.

Even with the privilege, most people lie to their attorneys. That's where the half-truths come in. Mostly, they are afraid you won't help them if they tell you everything. And they're right.

"The first person to lie to you in a case will probably be your client," said Dean Perry.

I started to walk home, but instead, I stepped out into the street and hailed a cab. That's one fabulous thing about San Francisco. Cabs are everywhere so long as you are in a somewhat commercial area. And you can hail one with a wave of your arm.

"South Beach Harbor, please."

I knew I had no right to poke my nose into Sean's business. But everyone knows about Hello Kitties and curiosity. It was inevitable.

WHEN I ARRIVED AT South Beach Harbor, I walked over to Gate E. Because I didn't have a gatekey, I couldn't go down to where the boats were docked. I waited by the gate for a minute or so, but the docks were deserted. Not a soul in sight.

So I ran back up the steps to the walkway terrace overlooking the boats. From where I stood, I counted to the thirteenth slip where *The Countess* should be docked. The slip stood silent and empty.

My left lower eyelid started pulsating rapidly. A bad omen.

According to Chinese superstition, if your upper eyelid flutters, it means a large feast is coming your way. If your lower eyelid flutters, find an exit strategy. Fast. It means trouble your way comes.

"Mom, my eyelid is jumping," I said, when it happened for the first time. I was in the third grade.

"Lower or upper lid?"

"Lower."

"Go splash some water on it. And say 'God forbid! God forbid! God forbid!'"

"What?"

"Fiona, just do as I say. Or something bad is going to happen."

Okay.

But three days later, my father still lost his job. The water splashing didn't kept the bad fortune at bay from our family.

That's the thing with omens. Dousing the messenger with water or flames isn't going to change what's coming. Neither is asking God to forbid it. Rather than burying your head in the sand, better to stay on your toes and be on your guard. Nothing else really works, no matter what your mother tells you.

As I walked through the harbor parking lot, my eyelid continued to pulsate. A hot, beating nerve twitched under the skin, filling me with a sense of doom despite my rational mind telling me the contrary.

I returned to the office to finish my work for the evening, keeping my cell phone on my desk and email open on my desktop.

But no Sean.

Contrary to what he said, we didn't meet up the next day, or the day after that. I waited for a phone call, text message, email—none of which came.

One good thing about being in Catholic school was that you had to account for all your absences. The Sisters of the Immaculate Conception didn't just mark you down as absent. They called your house and demanded to know why you weren't at school. Then on Monday mornings, you had to talk about what you did over the weekend in front of the whole class, unless you spent it blowing chunks or crapping your pants. You couldn't just disappear for days on end without a note or some kind of explanation.

No exceptions. Not even for Sean.

On Friday afternoon, I got a text message from Sean. Short, unobtrusive, and no need to be in front of the computer. For people on the go. I love text messages, even if AT&T charges me ten cents for each one.

Going to Tahoe for weekend. To try my luck. Drinks when I return.

I didn't reply as I felt a bit slighted that Sean didn't invite me up to Tahoe with him. My father had no dates planned for me, and my own plans for the weekend consisted of working, trying to rack up billable hours to build a comfortable cushion. In case I got sick, had an emergency, or just wanted a day or two off that year from Doreen. Or in case Saks Fifth Avenue had a huge one day sale.

No big deal.

It wouldn't hurt to show Doreen that I worked weekends. All lawyers are expected to work weekends. It's one of those rules they forget to mention in law school.

But that weekend, San Francisco got a bout of earthquake weather. Another bad omen.

Earthquake weather. That's what we call hot, humid, oppressive, cloudy conditions that occur in late September in the City by the Bay. Once upon a time, we enjoyed our Indian summers, especially after our chilly Julys and Augusts. But ever since the 1989 Loma Prieta quake, every time it gets hot in the city after Labor Day, we all get nervous. We stock up on bottled water, CLIF bars, Duracell batteries, first-aid kits. We get twitchy and paranoid, waiting for the next big one.

It's like waiting for the Second Coming. Seismologists have been promising the next Big One ever since 1906. That was the last big one. Then Loma Prieta hit. It wasn't big enough because it failed to turn San Francisco into a new Pacific island. So we are still waiting.

For Jesus and the Big One.

But instead of repenting for sins, my father sent me to Safeway to get bottled water and Wonder bread.

"Get the large family size, Fiona."

"I know, Dad."

Sean called while I was standing in the middle of the beverage aisle, deciding between Alhambra and Arrowhead.

"You're doing what, Fi?"

"Stocking up on water. This earthquake weather is making everyone uneasy."

"Right. It's been hot here."

"In Tahoe?"

"Uh, no, I'm back in the city."

"I thought you said you were going to be there for the whole weekend."

"Change of plans."

In the background, I heard the sounds of waves, seagulls, boats. Harbor music.

"Sean, where are you?"

"Oh, just out and about for an evening walk near my apartment." Which was nowhere near South Beach Harbor. "Fi, you want to grab a drink later on?"

"Sure. Aren't you tired after coming back from your trip?"

"What?"

"Aren't you tired after Tahoe?"

"Oh, no, I'm good. I just went up there briefly, did a little hiking, but got bored and came back."

"Hiking? Since when were you a nature lover?" I had trouble imagining Sean ruining his leather Italian loafers in the dirt and muck of Mother Nature.

Sean laughed. "Fi, have you ever been up there? Nice woods, great views. Lots of trails."

"No, I haven't. My cousins go for the skiing. And I'm not a skiier."

"Too bad. You'd like the lake. It's very clear and deep."

"You said you were going up there to try your luck. I assume you did a little gambling?"

"A little. Guess I was wrong. Luck's still with me. So you want to grab a drink or not, Fi?"

"Okay. Where?"

"Someplace in the Marina. How about the Matrix Fillmore? You know that place?"

"Oh yeah, lovely meat market with a giant fireplace in the

middle. I doubt they're going to have that going in this heat wave though."

"'Cuz we're going for the décor.'"

Right.

I returned home with a case of Arrowhead water, three loaves of Wonder bread, a dozen cartons of Stouffer's meals, and Sean's half-truths. I knew he loved sailing, but he hated hiking ever since he learned about ticks in health class.

"You're just asking to get lyme disease," he said once.

Maybe Sean had changed his mind about ticks, about nature. Maybe he was up at Lake Tahoe in the woods. Maybe he wasn't. All I did know was he had been away and near a body of water.

I told myself it didn't really matter.

The oppressive, muggy heat—a sign of an impending quake— lifted two days later and San Franciscans breathed a huge sigh of relief. The wait for the Big One would continue.

On Monday afternoon, Caroline Derby's bloated, fish-nibbled body washed up on the shores of San Francisco Bay.

Then everything mattered.

For the first time, Sean was wrong. His luck had begun to run out.

CHAPTER
TWENTY-ONE

S EAN HATED OVERSEXED WOMEN and bullies. That much I knew. But why he did what he did during his night outings, I could only guess. Maybe he wanted to make the world a better place. Maybe he did it for the thrill.

Like Brenda Spencer, who shot up a San Diego schoolyard because she just didn't like Mondays.

So no one *really* knows. Not even FBI profilers. They just label such murders simply as thrill kills. Because most serial killers enjoy doing God's work. And it's fun, like torturing Jesus and blowing a wet raspberry at the police for being donut-eating, coffee-chugging dumbasses.

Problem is that you have to survive to keep doing God's work. In order to be prolific like the Green River Killer, you have to be out and about in free society, mixing with your potential victims, not behind bars. Getting captured would be a career-ending move.

But even for the best of the best, "All good things must come to an end," as the old English proverb says. You make a mistake.

Someone sees you. You leave something behind. And it all ends. You get your bunk on Death Row, especially if you did God's work in California.

Or your luck just runs out. Simple as that. Some beagle goes digging where it shouldn't. Landslides regurgitate your skeletons onto the public sidewalk. Strong currents and waves sweep your secrets up from the bottom of the sea and cast them ashore. Then everyone knows.

For Sean, things began to unravel after the discovery of Caroline's body.

CAROLINE DERBY. RICH, single, white, young. Now too pretty and too dead. She spent her last night alive bar hopping, hoping to meet her soulmate over a bellini or two. Instead, she met her Maker after leaving with an attractive white man who according to various inebriated eyewitnesses, looked a lot like Pierce Brosnan, Brad Pitt, and Benicio Del Toro.

Good luck with that description, SFPD.

But the media became fascinated by the dead girl with the lovely cheekbones and dirty blonde hair. Dead Barbie washing up like kelp was definitely newsworthy. So the media ran about a dozen stories warning young women about roofies and going out to bars alone.

Thanks to Caroline, the young women all stayed home.

Sean's hunting trips at the ritzy bars were on hiatus, so instead we went for a long, evening drive through various parts of the City.

We drove to the Tenderloin, San Francisco's red light district, and studied the ladies of the night in their vinyl mini skirts, fishnet stockings, platform stilettos, faux fur wraps, cheap makeup. All oozing sex appeal.

I double-checked that the passenger side door was locked properly, unlocking and locking the button on the armrest of Sean's Mercedes.

"No worries, Fi. You're fine," Sean said without looking over.

Despite the sketchy neighborhood, a part of me never felt safer than when I was with Sean. Perhaps that was why I agreed to accompany him to the bars. And why I was with him in the car. No one would dare tickle me anywhere. Not with Sean around.

"Sean, let's go and have a drink at the Big Four."

"Big Four?"

"Old, rich geezer bar at the Huntington."

"I know where it is, Fi. I was just surprised that you suggested that place."

"It's nice, quiet, and full of rich, white people. And safe."

"Oh, you know you're safe with me. I'll take you home after you do your part."

He was right. "My part?"

"Don't piss your undies. You're an amoeba, I know. I just want you to help me with the selection."

"I see."

Some serial killers kill to clean up the scourge of the earth. They get rid of vermin like drug dealers, pimps, child molesters. People whose depravity has already condemned them to early deaths.

More power to these self-appointed guardians of morality.

But Sean targeted prostitutes now because his supply of classy, snooty women dried up thanks to Caroline Derby.

"You don't need me, Sean."

"No, but it's more fun this way. For both of us."

Sean might be out of luck, but he was still right. It's always more fun to do things with a friend.

I spotted a tall, black girl with Tina Turner hair wearing a red spandex top with a plunging sweetheart neckline. Silver spangled mini skirt. No stockings. For easy access. And red patent leather stilettos.

"This is my corner, ho! You get the hell off my corner," she screamed at another girl who looked terrified. She started swinging her big purse at her competition. The other girl finally ran away.

"That one," I said as we drove by her corner.

"Why?"

"You know why." Because she is a big sex pot as well as a big bully.

Sean glanced over and nodded approvingly.

"Very good, Fi. Now pick another."

"What?"

"A second one."

"Sean, take it easy."

"You're no fun. Okay, home you go. It's good you live so close."

I do. I live in a large, comfortable Nob Hill flat with my parents for basically a fraction of the market rent, thanks to rent control.

Sean dropped me off and sped back to the Tenderloin. As I watched his red tail lights disappear into the dark night, my stomach knotted up with a bad feeling.

Overconfidence, overreaching arrogance, pride, refusal to heed warnings. That's why Icarus fell.

I told myself Sean would be fine. No one was smarter, more careful, calculating. He would be all right.

I HAD SOMETHING NEW to face at home.

"That is terrible. Why would she ask him to do such a thing?" my mother said as I walked through the door.

My parents were huddled together at the dining table, deep in discussion. My father turned when I came in.

"Who do what thing, Mom?"

"Your cousin, Katie. Who lives in L.A."

"Yes, I remember Katie." Katie who told me I needed to bleach my face and to lose weight. Katie who flaunted her young Chinese husband in my face the last time I visited her. "What about her?"

"She doesn't want to have children."

"So Katie isn't that dumb after all."

"Fiona, I'm serious. She wants Peter to be unable to have kids."

"She wants him to have an operation," clarified my father.

Snip snip. Poor Peter. Guess he didn't fancy the idea of being neutered. "Just tell them to stock up on rubbers."

"Fiona! Don't be crude!" my mother said.

"I'm not. I'm being practical."

"We don't understand why she doesn't want kids. Katie is Chinese. Hong Kong born. I don't understand why she would ask him to do such a thing. He's such a nice boy," moaned my mother.

Because Katie has had a taste of America.

Because she likes her life the way it is and doesn't want it to change. And Hello Kitty didn't want a kitten turning her firm boobs into swinging pendulums.

I understood my mother's confusion. Chinese folks love children. After all, that's why they scatter peanuts all over the bedspread of the wedding bed. As many descendants as there are peanuts. And the Cantonese word for "peanuts" even sounds like the word for "giving birth."

Children are wonderful. Especially male children. Sons, sons, sons. Even though there can be no sons without daughters, everyone still prefers sons. They don't think about who their sons are going to marry when they grow up.

Logical gymnastics.

According to some customs, a wife can't even eat dinner at the dinner table with the family unless she has given birth to a son. She has not made herself worthy to them.

"Mom, Dad, it's simple. Katie's getting ready to divorce Peter."

"That's ridiculous. Divorce! Don't even say it."

"Let's face it. Peter needed a green card. Katie wanted the money. That's the only reason he put up with Katie's crap. And why she put up with his. She's not going to stay married to him forever."

"Katie is a good girl. She wants to have children."

No she doesn't. She wants to send Peter under the knife. Because she knows that that kids would just chain her to him forever.

I never liked Peter. I thought of him as little better than a green card whore, which he was. His family paid Katie's mom forty thousand dollars to put him up for a semester when he got into UC Berkeley. Or so she said.

I never liked Katie. I thought of her as little better than a money whore, which she was. A money whore who was obsessed with skin whiteners and diet pills.

A few months later, Peter and Katie got married at a Las Vegas wedding chapel. No disgruntled bridesmaids. No reception. No three-tiered wedding cake. No engagement ring. But Katie got a brand new eighty-thousand-dollar Lexus.

After spending some time with the newlyweds, I found that I actually felt sorry for the both of them. I realized they had to put up with each other.

"So what do you guys do on the weekends?" I asked Peter one afternoon when Katie was out.

"We go shopping at Target, clean up the apartment, go shopping downtown. That kind of thing."

"Why don't you go on romantic vacations together?"

"No money. Katie went to Europe by herself."

"What?"

"Katie took a tour of Europe."

"Why didn't you go with her?"

"We didn't have the money for two people to go, so she went by herself."

Okay.

"So what did you do at home, Peter?"

"Fixed up the house, waited for her."

Christ.

Then Peter had to deal with Katie's temper tantrums and her mother's endless demands around the house, rides to and from here and there, grocery trips. He became the designated grocery boy, chauffeur, cook, handyman. And now he wanted to be a father.

But Katie wasn't interested in motherhood. She wanted other things.

No wonder the poor guy wanted out.

"Mom, Katie treats him like crap. She's a bully."

"She has a temper, I know."

"And now she wants him to get snipped."

My mother didn't say anything for a moment. She mulled her thoughts over and finally threw her hands up in frustration.

"You know, forget it! Don't listen to your father's silliness anymore, Fiona."

"What?"

"Getting married and all that. Go live your life. Buy yourself some more Dior shoes, kiss Pepito, have a great life."

Hai, Mom.

"It's not worth it. Look at Katie. Young people these days! A good Chinese girl telling her husband to make himself unable to have babies at his age. You're right, Fiona. She wants to divorce him."

"Divorce is better than ending up headless in some ditch, Mom."

"Don't say that."

"It's true. Tell Katie to get herself a good attorney."

But Peter ended up being the one who needed a lawyer.

About a month later, the LAPD arrested Peter when my aunt found Katie lying at the bottom of the stairs with a broken neck. The couple had been arguing upstairs. About having babies. About not having babies.

The neighbors heard them. My aunt heard them. Next thing everyone knew, Katie tumbled down the stairs. Peter claimed she had tripped over her nightgown. My aunt said he pushed her.

So LAPD arrested him for murder.

Welcome to America. Peter would be staying. And he didn't even need a green card.

As for Katie, she got a free trip to the morgue. Because that's what happens to Hello Kitties who don't play by the rules. You don't do what your parents tell you, you get put out. You don't have children when your husband wants children, you end up with a broken neck.

And Katie's CPA degree and designer shoe collection didn't do shit to prevent her trip down the stairs.

Katie's death made me think about Don. About how I had saved myself from a similar fate. It was him or me. There was no other way, unless I wanted to join my cousin at the Medical Examiner's office. Not a good place. They don't serve fifteen-dollar bellinis there.

"See, Dad? Katie should have just divorced him. It would have been better than a broken neck."

"You were right."

"What?"

"You were right about Peter. Poor Katie."

"See? Stop trying to set me up with Peters. I like my neck the way it is."

I thought my father was going to chastize me for my comment, but he didn't. Instead, he laughed.

"Me too, Fiona."

Me three.

CHAPTER
TWENTY-TWO

SEAN'S CAR SMELLED FUNNY. Not like dead squirrels, but like peach orchards, pine cones, vanilla mint, ocean breeze, citrus medley. An olfactory rainbow of air fresheners.

But not even the combined efforts of Glade, Lysol, and Febreeze could mask the cheap perfumes worn by Sean's recently deceased passengers.

"Dude, pick one scent and stick with it," I told him.

"What?"

"Your car. It smells like vanilla citrus ocean breeze."

"That's good."

As long as it didn't smell like dead squirrels or dead hookers, Sean didn't care. Because he couldn't smell it anyway.

Sean began picking up a lot of prostitutes in his fancy Mercedes. They took one look at him and the car and went to their doom willingly. It became too easy.

I hoped he would get sick of his new pastime. Instead, he became addicted.

I learned this when he took me with him on the weekends, after I had finished Doreen's work. We went to bars, had fifteen-dollar drinks, and went for drives through hooker country.

"How's Doreen?"

"Still alive and giving me assignments."

"Too bad. You can't come along for more fun with your buddy."

"More fun?"

Sean said nothing. We drove by several women in mini-mini skirts and platform fuck-me shoes. They jeered at us, waving their arms.

"I do couples, honey!" one yelled after us.

I turned and looked at Sean, who kept his eyes on the road like a good driver. Always thinking of the safety of others, Sean was.

"Hear that? She sounds like your kind of fun."

"Nah."

"Why not?"

"The last one was black. Two days ago."

"Two days ago?"

"Yeah, sorry, Fi. Couldn't wait for you to come along."

"So this one is no good?"

"She's black too. Never develop too much of a type or pattern. Just cuts your career short."

Right.

So we drove around some more until Sean spotted a redhead in a black leather skirt and pink boa scarf with a big hair-sprayed updo. She was cussing at a car that refused to pick her up. "Go home and suck your momma's titties," she yelled, shaking her heavy chest.

"Now that's my type of girl, Fi."

"A redhead?"

"Mean and nasty."

Sean pulled over to the curb right in front of her, but before he lowered the passenger side window he said, "No worries, Fi. I'll drop you off at Big Four. Wait for me there?"

"What are you doing?"

"No worries, Fi. Trust me. Tonight will be a blast."

The girl bent over and peered in at us through the lowered window, giving me a dirty look. I ignored her, staring straight ahead.

"Sorry, guys. I don't do couples," she said, winding her gum around her finger before popping it back in her mouth.

"Nah, I'm dropping this one off. How would you like to spend a night at the Mark Hopkins?"

"Mark Hopkins?"

"Yeah, get in."

And she did.

Sean dropped me off a block away from the bar and winked as I slammed the door closed. The hooker sneered at me from the back seat. I felt uneasy, especially because Sean had passed me off as a prostitute.

I wondered what Sean had in mind. Taking the girl to a place like the Mark Hopkins where the doorman or bellhop would remember them. Risky, stupid, out of character for Sean.

I watched as they drove off. I watched the car go right past the Mark Hopkins, disappearing down a hill towards the bay. The red tail lights of his Mercedes flashed like demonic eyes from the movies.

I wasn't so sure that this girl deserved what she was going to get. She just wanted to make a living. It was her body, her life, her choice of profession. In California, if you've got it, you flaunt it, market it, sell it. All to the highest bidder. Just ask the folks in Hollywood. It's West Coast culture.

I suspected that it no longer mattered to Sean. Whether someone was asking for it or not. He was in it for the thrill now. I prayed that he was not devolving, throwing caution to the wind, giving in completely to the darkness. Because that would lead him straight to San Quentin State Prison.

I walked into the Big Four and sat down at a small table. I took out my cell phone and kept it in front of me.

"What can I get you?" asked a waitress with a Russian accent.

"A glass of riesling, please."

And a glass of cabernet.

About an hour and a half later, Sean called. I jumped when my cell phone began flashing and vibrating.

"Ever been sailing at night?"

"Do people even go sailing at night, Sean?"

"Pick you up in a bit."

He hung up without waiting for my answer.

Being on the water at night seemed creepy and unnatural to me. Almost like flying a kite at night in the rain. So of course, I had to go.

"Want anything else, miss?"

"Yes, a strong cup of coffee."

Whatever Sean had in mind, I wanted to be clear-minded and awake, in case I needed to be. The waitress brought me coffee. I drank it black in quick little sips, hoping to get all the caffeine in me I could before Sean pulled up.

We drove down to South Beach Harbor. It was deserted. But walking with Sean, I was fearless. Nothing feels safer than walking around with the most dangerous man in town.

"It's a calm night, Fi. Thought you'd like to go for a midnight sail."

"So long as you don't steer us into a bridge."

Sean laughed.

When we sailed past Ghirardelli Square, he handed the tiller over to me. Ghirardelli Square is home to the Ghirardelli Chocolate Factory and the Ghirardelli Soda Fountain & Chocolate Shop, known for its world famous ice cream sundaes which I have never tried, believing, like many residents, that I can do so at any time. But tourists flock to it at Fisherman's Wharf in droves.

"Isn't Ghirardelli Square spectacular at nighttime?" Sean asked, his eyes sparkling.

"I've never seen it look so pretty before. I can't take my eyes off of it."

And I didn't.

I kept my eyes on the glittering lights of the Wharf, the dark shapes of houses, trees, cars below the huge Ghirardelli sign, while Sean shuffled around in the shadows behind me. He was moving objects on the starboard side, partially hidden by the main sail.

Splash.

Sean had pushed something over the side of the boat.

I ignored the sound. "Have you ever been to that restaurant at the top of Ghirardelli Square, Sean?"

"No, is it any good?"

Splash.

"Remember Laurie from my old firm? She said that place has the best strawberry milkshakes."

"You like milkshakes, Fi?"

Sean kicked at something with his foot. It rolled over and fell into the water. Splash.

"No, I hate milkshakes. It's like drinking snot. Strawberry ones are the worst. They're Liquid Tylenol-flavored snot."

He laughed. "Then we won't go to that restaurant."

"Sean, I'm hungry. I had too much wine at the Big Four. I need some food."

"What's open this hour?"

"Chinatown restaurants. I know a great one."

"Cool. I'm getting cold anyway. Let's turn back into the harbor."

So we did.

COLD AND WET, WE arrived at Yuet Lee, a cheap seafood restaurant in Chinatown that stayed open into the wee hours of the night.

I ordered jook, Chinese breakfast rice soup. But this savory rice porridge is not only for breakfast. It's perfect for a midnight meal and for curing the common cold. It's our version of chicken soup. It's soul food, especially if you add a little seafood, pork, and slices of pickled egg.

A satisfying meal for anyone after a hard night of doing God's work.

"So what do you have planned for the holidays, Fi?"

"Well, next week, I have Katie's funeral in L.A. Then I might stay down there to see what becomes of poor Peter."

"Sounds like fun. But who's going to take care of your bird?"

If I was away from Pepito for too long, he would feed me his doughnuts as punishment for ditching him. Or worse yet, he would die of neglect. "Crap. Nevermind. I'll just go for the funeral. Knowing my aunt, it'll be a full-blown Chinese affair. In other words, it'll just suck."

"Don't they serve Peking duck or shark fin soup at the wake?"

"You wish. It's cheap Chinese food."

"Maybe you'll get lucky and they'll do it American style."

I RETURNED HOME LATE. My parents had left the hallway light on for me. I love them.

"You want some hot water?" my mother asked. She had heard me come in.

Boiled water. Healthy boiled water with only dead bacteria.

"No thanks, Mom. I'm going to bed."

"Okay."

She didn't even ask where I had been or whether I was drunk. Guess Katie's death convinced her to let me have some fun.

Because poor Katie didn't. She got married and got killed. No fun.

Too bad Katie didn't live here and use our Laundromat. I could have done her and Peter a big favor. I could have saved her life with a pair of lacy panties or a cherry lipstick smear.

But thanks to her, I would get a couple of days in Los Angeles.

"Remember not to mention anything about Peter, Fiona," my father instructed me on the plane.

Duh. Like he really needed to tell me not to talk about Peter at Katie's funeral. A total no-brainer.

"And don't speak to Peter's family," my mother said.

"Peter's family is going to be there?"

"Yes, they flew over from Hong Kong yesterday."

To be with their son while he went on trial for murdering his wife.

"Is Peter going to be there, Mom?"

"I don't think so. I think the police still have him."

Oh.

"Fiona, did you bring one of your nice suits?"

"No, Mom. I brought a cheap skirt and blouse." In case we had to torch my outfit so Death didn't come home with us.

"Did you bring shoes?"

"Yes."

"And hose?"

"Yes."

"Good girl."

My father remained quiet until the plane landed. When we got off the plane, he turned to me, looking as if he just remembered something.

"And Fiona."

"Yeah?"

"Remember to wear lipstick."

CHAPTER
TWENTY-THREE

K ATIE LAY IN A SHINY COFFIN, looking like an anorexic geisha in a purple Zac Posen dress.

She would have loved the way she looked. Of that, I was certain. The mortician did a fantastic job with her pasty makeup. Saint Peter would not be able to chastize her for being too dark or too fat when she arrived at the Pearly Gates. If she was any whiter or thinner, he would be welcoming a skeleton in a kabuki mask.

Aunt Lydia spared us the horrors of a customary Chinese burial so she could openly mourn her daughter. God bless the woman. I would not have to burn my clothes.

But the manner of Katie's death ruined all the good energies of her All-American funeral for me. Instead of the usual grief and satisfaction, anger hung in the heavily-scented air of the funeral home. Hatred and resentment oozed from the pores of Katie and Peter's families.

"Don't look at them," my father whispered.

"I'm not."

"Don't talk to them."

"They're not even looking at us, Dad."

"So don't look at them."

"I'm not. I'm looking at my shoes."

"Go sit next to Aunt Lydia while I talk with your uncle."

I didn't want to sit next to Aunt Lydia, who was crying and seething with bad energy, but I did so anyway.

"I'm so sorry for your loss, Aunt Lydia."

"Thank you, Fiona. You are such a good girl."

Uh huh. Of course I am.

So I sat there next to my aunt in front of Katie's coffin until a fight broke out in the waiting room next door. Aunt Lydia sprang to her feet and joined in.

"Your son killed my daughter!"

"No, he didn't. It was an accident."

"It was no accident! He pushed her!"

"She was clumsy. She tripped over her own feet. It's not his fault."

"Of course it's his fault!"

"She was a terrible wife!"

"What? She was wonderful to him. And he murdered her!"

"If she was so great, they wouldn't have fought, and she'd still be alive!"

I got up and sauntered into the waiting room for a peek. My uncle thrashed his arms at someone cowering in a corner. My father held him back. A woman shielded the other man from my uncle.

"Fiona, go back in the other room."

Hai, Daddy.

But I didn't.

I wandered off to explore the other rooms of the funeral home, leaving the fight behind.

"Excuse me, where is the ladies' room?" I asked a young woman in the front office.

"That way, to your right."

I love checking out the restrooms at restaurants, hotels, funeral homes. Restrooms tell you a lot about a place and the people who work there. Whether they value cleanliness, aesthetics, utility, atmosphere, décor, quality. Because restrooms aren't the first things patrons see. They're the places where you can skimp or neglect. And most places do.

It's like people who dress up to the nines but go around in dirty underwear or with untrimmed toenails. No one can see those things. So they don't care.

The funeral home's bathroom smelled like lemons. Plain, but clean and cheery with its baby yellow tiles. A large bouquet of daisies in a clear glass vase sat on a whitewashed wooden stand. Even the hand soap had a citrus scent. The stalls boasted clean walls, toilets which had a powerful flush, and plenty of toilet seat covers and quilted toilet paper. The floors were free of paper towels.

We are a no-nonsense, practical, cheery, and sanitary funeral home. Clean like lemons. That's what the bathroom said.

Shouting voices assaulted me as I stepped out of the peaceful bathroom. My uncle and Peter's parents were still fighting. Their voices carried down the carpeted hallway.

"I hope your son rots in jail!"

"I hope your daughter rots in hell!"

So I kept exploring.

At the end of the hall, a large sign read "RESTRICTED." Morticians prepared the dead for their big day beyond that point. It would be rude to walk in on the dead in their indecent state while they were getting a manicure or haircut.

I wondered if the morticians gave their clients pedicures. After all, no one would ever know.

Urns. A whole table full of them stood in a room on my right. Marble, silver, gold, porcelain. You name it. Different sizes, different shapes with little tags on them.

SYLVIA LYNN BRETON

NORMAN JERROLD KRAMER

BURT ALAN SMITH

I switched all the name tags around. Ashes to ashes. It's all the same. Might as well send them all on a final adventure. Never too late to have some fun.

Farewell, Sylvia.

Rest in peace, Norman.

Godspeed, Burt.

"You are not supposed to be in here."

The funeral director, a middle-aged Chinese man wearing a black suit and gray tie, stood at the entrance of the room.

"Oh, sorry, I got lost. I'm waiting for my cousin's service to begin."

"This way, miss."

Katie's funeral service put everyone in a foul mood. We sat on one side of the room. Peter's family sat on the other. My delicate porous psyche suffered from the terrible mounting tension. Not even the delicious pecan pie at the wake could dispel the tidal wave of bad energy.

Still, I helped myself to two slices. And talked to the two homicide detectives who attended Katie's funeral. I failed to realize their presence until one of them approached me, interrupting my second slice of pie.

"Were you a friend of Katie's?"

"Cousin."

"I'm sorry for your loss. I'm Detective Dubler. I'm looking into your cousin's death. That guy over there is my partner."

Detective Dubler. Big, tall, white guy. Ex-military build. Moustache. Middle-aged. Definitely not green and not too jaded to get after the truth.

"You mind if I ask you a few questions?"

"Sure. Why not? I'm Fiona."

"Fiona, were you close to your cousin?"

"Not really. I live in San Francisco. I only visited her a couple of times. L.A. is not my kind of town."

"I understand. Did you know her husband, Peter?"

"About as well as I knew my cousin."

"Did they get along?"

"I don't know really."

"So you never heard about any issues that they might have had?"

"Detective, every couple has issues. But no one's died until now."

"Did Peter ever lose his temper or become violent?"

"I wouldn't know. But then again, I wasn't married to him. He had to be nice and polite to me."

Detective Dubler chuckled and then quickly recomposed himself. He was at the wake of a possible murder victim, after all.

"Fiona, you don't seem very upset that your cousin is dead."

"Like I said, we weren't very close. And she wasn't that nice to me the few times I visited her."

"No? Now why is that?"

"Just a tad bit snooty. NorCal girl versus SoCal girl kind of thing."

"Was she ever snooty with Peter?"

"Dunno. You'll have to ask him."

"What about your aunt? Did she like Peter?"

"She liked him enough to let him marry Katie, but beyond that, I don't know. Ask her."

"Okay, thank you, Fiona. And again, I'm sorry for your loss."

"You really don't think this was an accident, do you, Detective?"

"I don't know about that. I do know that they were arguing right before Katie died."

Right.

And because most of the time, it's not an accident. Just like Don Koo, Nicole Brown Simpson, Laci Peterson. I couldn't blame Detective Dubler for not thinking otherwise.

"One more thing, Fiona. Did Katie ever talk about whether she wanted children?"

"Not to me."

Short and sweet. A good rule of thumb for speaking with the police. Never go into a narrative or tell them how you hated your cousin for calling you dark and fat. Or how she had been asking for it, just like Don had been asking for it. They'll think you had something to do with the death. Or worse yet, they might think you're a valuable witness. Then you're really screwed.

224

"POLICE ARE NOTHING BUT trouble, unless you need them," Sean said when I returned from my Katie's funeral. "Avoid until needed."

"I'll drink to that."

"At least your trip wasn't boring, Fi."

"Nope, between the fight and the police, it proved quite exciting."

"Good."

"What have you been up to, Sean?"

"Nothing much."

Actually he had been very busy.

Sean had become deeply addicted to his nightly work. By the time Thanksgiving rolled around, whenever I called in the evenings for dinner or drinks, I only got his voicemail. Then a few hours later, he would invite me sailing despite the freezing weather. Every time.

He was in the groove now and he didn't want anything to disrupt the rhythm of his deadly dance. So I became a liability. He stopped taking me with me on his nightly drives. "Having to take you home ruins the mood, Fi."

Soon the whispers began. As more and more hookers disappeared off the streets, people started talking. It was as if the City suddenly realized that some of its inhabitants had evaporated into thin air. It felt lighter, roomier, cleaner. And the change wasn't due to any efforts by the mayor.

The credit lay elsewhere.

Rumors began spreading about a serial killer on the loose in the Bay Area. Like the Zodiac Killer.

The City waited for cryptic notes to be sent to the San Francisco Chronicle or The Examiner. The media waited for mysterious packages to be mailed to NBC, ABC, CBS. Even to FOX. The police prepared for taunting phone calls and puzzle boxes.

But nothing came.

Everyone continued to wait. And the prostitutes continued to disappear off the streets.

The police got tired of prostitutes and pimps streaming into the stations reporting missing colleagues, pretending that the missing woman was their friend, or a friend of a friend. After all, no pimp was going to walk up to the desk sergeant and say, "Hey, man, my ho didn't show up on her corner," or, "Hey, I'm missing a ho." But still, in the end, their visits generated too many reports that needed to be filed. Too much paperwork. So they doubled the number of patrol cars in the Tenderloin, bringing the number up to two.

"Maybe the weather got too cold for them and they went to L.A."

"Those mini skirts sure aren't too warm."

"Chapped lips are a bitch. Upstairs and downstairs."

So I imagined the one-liners being exchanged in the police cruisers.

As word spread, Sean stayed home more often. The risk of exposure forced him to take a break. So instead he invited me over for dinner and drinks at his place, but his attention drifted elsewhere.

No feather boa. No light-hearted banter. No fun.

"Go beat the baby if I'm boring you, Fi."

Even the big punching bag baby hung still and unmolested while storms brewed inside of Sean.

He paced back and forth in front of the television, drink in hand. I sat on the couch, watching him. Like a caged animal slowly going crazy from boredom, he started biting his lower lip and rubbing his chin. He tried to wear a smooth patch on the hardwood floor. Until he couldn't stand it any longer.

"Fi, go home. I need to get to work."

So I went home.

Never get between a man and his work. People culture.

TWENTY-FOUR

PETER'S CASE NEVER MADE it to trial. Out on bail, he hung himself in the bathroom one night, after his parents had gone to bed. They found his body the next morning.

"We're not going to his funeral," declared my father. "Aunt Lydia is not going. So we don't have to."

"I'm not surprised, Dad. He killed Katie."

The police took Peter's suicide as a confession of guilt. Peter's parents took it as a proclamation of his innocence—an act of desperation to escape the endless accusations. Unfortunately, if that had been his true motivation, the plan backfired. Most people took his death the same way the police did.

Peter should have left a note. But he didn't.

"He just couldn't face the jail time, Fi," Sean told me.

"I don't blame him. Not a fun place to go."

"Nope. No more Armani or bellinis."

"No."

"And all the butt sex you never wanted. Think of all the action

Petey missed out on."

The murder-suicide reinforced my father's decision to stop pressuring me about marriage. Thanks, Peter.

I HOPED PETER'S SUICIDE would persuade Sean to give up his night job. It didn't. I wondered what he would do if he ever got caught.

"If you were Peter, would you have killed yourself?" I asked.

"Never."

Sean took a swig of his beer, tucked his arm behind his head, and continued staring at the television. We were watching *South Park* episodes on DVD and snacking on nachos and beer. It was still early in the evening.

"You would have gone to trial, Sean?"

"And gotten off."

"It didn't work for Bundy or Unterweger, you know."

"Losers."

No, they weren't. They were among the elite of psychopathic serial killers. And their charm still failed them at trial.

Sean's arrogance made me uneasy. I wanted to discourage him from ramping up his nightly activities, but I knew it would be useless. He was on a roll. He knew it. I knew it. Even though we both knew it couldn't last forever.

"Okay, ten o'clock, Fi. Home you go."

"And you?"

"I'm a big boy, Fi. None of your business."

At least Sean told me nicely. Every time I asked my grandmother a question that I shouldn't have, she said, "And how many pubic hairs do you have down there?" It was her way of saying "none of your business." God bless her.

Every evening, Sean and I met up for drinks or dinner and shot the breeze. Every night, he sent me home. I told myself it was because he was looking out for me. That if anything should go wrong, I would not end up in prison for the rest of my life as his accomplice before or after the fact.

But I knew better.

Sean considered himself several leagues above me now. I became the annoying little sister tagging along on her big brother's important adult business. He didn't need me to help him pick out his girls anymore. He wanted to do it himself.

So I spent my nights at home.

Or more often at the office, late into the night, plodding through my financing agreements and merger contracts with only a pixilated portrait of the Blood Countess for company.

Eventually, I stopped hearing from Sean altogether. No calls, no emails, no text messages. No bar hopping, no drinks and nachos, no sailing trips. No Sean.

All the modern technology in the world could not bridge the growing gap between Sean and me. He had moved on and left me behind. Like the friends you outgrow when you go onto something bigger and better.

It's all part of life, unless of course, you're the friend left behind. Then it just plain sucks.

I found myself wishing for Sean to slip up.

And then he did.

ALL IT TAKES IS ONE survivor. The one who gets away. And runs off to the police with your description and a story about what you tried to do to them. Like what happened with Dahmer.

Dahmer lucked out with his first escapee. The oh-so-helpful cops who lived to serve and protect actually delivered the poor guy back to Dahmer, who could have gone on happily killing and eating boys and men if his last would-be victim hadn't escaped. The guy went straight to the cops about his misadventure, and next thing Dahmer knew, a fellow inmate at the Columbia Correctional Institution, a man named Scarver, was bashing his skull in with a weight bar. Scarver said he was doing "the work of God."

Aren't we all.

My mother called me one night while I was at the office. "Fiona, come home early."

"I can't. I have lots of work, Mom."

"Have you seen the news?"

"You know I hate the news."

"There's a serial killer loose in the city. Lots of young women have been disappearing."

"Really?"

"Come home early. Can't you do your work at home?"

"I guess."

"Then come home. And read the news. They put up a picture of him in the news."

"A picture?"

I logged onto the Internet faster than ever before. Although I had been wishing for Sean to be exposed, I felt nauseous, hoping that the picture wasn't of him.

But it was. Sort of.

SFGate.com showed a sketch of the man who allegedly tried to kidnap and kill a young woman. The sketch looked like a bad cross between Edward Norton and Orlando Bloom, bearing only a slight resemblance to Sean.

Maybe that's what Sean looked like if you had enough roofies and alcohol in you. I wouldn't know. The only part of the sketch that had him dead on was a cold, slightly crooked sneer. I had seen that look too many times over the years, dating all the way back to the day he set Stephanie's head on fire.

The article read:

Attempted Kidnapping of Young San Francisco Woman: A young woman narrowly escaped a kidnapping attempt last night in the San Francisco Tenderloin District while walking home after drinking at a local bar with friends. A man tried to pull the young woman into his car while she stood at the corner waiting for the light. Police are distributing this sketch of the suspect who is believed to be a Caucasian male between the ages of twenty-five and forty...

Like I said, it's always a white guy between the ages of twenty-five and forty. Unless it's some random drive-by shooting in Oakland.

The article continued with a discussion of how young women need to be more careful and aware of their surroundings while walking around at night, how police are investigating the incident, how to contact the police if anyone should recognize the man in the sketch.

I laughed when I read the part about how the young woman was standing at the corner waiting for the light. Newspaper half-truths. No one would give a crap if they had said the woman was a hooker looking for her next John. People would just say she was asking for something like that to happen.

The next day, I called Sean at his office.

"Dr. Killroy is in surgery."

"When will he be out?"

"I don't know. Would you like to leave a message?"

"Please tell him Fiona called."

"Regarding what?"

"I need a new hymen."

I figured that might pique Sean's interest enough to call me back. He must have had a lot of hymen surgeries lined up. He didn't call me until a day and half later.

"Don't tell me your dad is making you get married again."

"No, Sean. I just needed to talk to you. Have you read the news lately?"

"No, too busy. Why?"

"You're on the front page. Sort of. Actually, the news isn't really about you. It's about the girl who got away."

Sean was silent for a very long time. At last, he spoke.

"Aw shit, Fi."

"Shit indeed, man."

"Listen, uh, I gotta go. Can you come over later this evening?"

"Sure."

Having his failure plastered over the front page of the Chronicle must have deflated Sean's ego somewhat. All of a sudden, I became worthy company once again. The part of me half in fear of Sean warned me against going over to his apartment.

But the part of me half in love with Sean worried about him, what would happen if someone recognized him, what would happen if he was captured and convicted, what would happen to him in prison.

The latter part won out.

Around seven o'clock, I buzzed Sean's apartment. Apartment 312. I wondered if he knew Dahmer's notorious apartment had been number 213. Maybe. I myself hadn't realized it until now.

Sean opened the door, not in his usual flamboyant, confident style, but more reserved and cautious. He peered down the hall to see if anyone else was watching.

"Fi, come in."

"It's okay. I don't think Betty is watching."

Sean said nothing for a minute as he swallowed a couple of times, running his fingers through his dark hair nervously.

"Oh, don't worry. She isn't."

I ignored the ominous tone in his voice, trying to keep my attitude as light and upbeat as possible.

"So I take it you saw the sketch, then?"

"It doesn't really look like me."

"True. They should fire that sketch artist."

"Apparently, he was good enough."

"What do you mean?"

Sean walked over to his liquor tray and began fixing me a drink. He dropped several ice cubes onto the ground.

"Shit."

Sean stooped over, picked up the ice and threw it back into the metal bucket.

"Sean, did someone recognize you?"

"Yeah, you could say that."

"Oh my God. Who?"

"Guess."

Sean's eyes twinkled, testing my astuteness. He dared me to read his mind, to prove that I was worthy to be his friend.

"No!"

"Yup."

"Betty?"

"You are a smart girl, Fi."

"Crap."

"Ye of little faith."

"What are you going to do, Sean? Oh God, nevermind. I don't want to know."

"Don't you?"

"You already did it." I spoke my realization aloud.

"What? You think I should have let the old gal run to the police?"

"Of course not, Sean. How did you know, anyway?"

"Believe it or not, she actually came over with the sketch in hand and accused me. Then she gloated about how she was going to tell the police."

"You're fucking kidding me."

"Nope."

"Stupid old cow."

"Never knew anyone to ask for it that much."

I had to laugh. Betty would never do anything so stupid again. Ever. You never go over to a suspected killer's place and brag about how you're planning to turn him in to the police. Dumb.

I flopped down onto Sean's couch, taking the drink he handed me without even caring what it was. I wrapped my hands around the cool glass and tried to focus. He had fixed me a scotch on the rocks. Suddenly, I wondered if he had added a sprinkle of roofies. I decided not to find out.

"I need to use the restroom," I said, setting down my drink on the coffee table.

"Uh, the bathroom is backed up at the moment." Sean blocked my way.

I looked at him.

Sean smiled and winked at me. Like he had done a million times before.

Betty.

I didn't have to go into Sean's bathroom to know that she was in there. Probably in the bathtub, waiting for him to dispose of her body at the first opportunity. The night was still young. Too many people out.

"I guess I don't really have to go right now."

"Good girl."

"So what are your plans for the evening, Sean?"

"I'm planning to stay in for a while, but I might go out for a stroll by the water later on."

"Cool. It's a nice night out."

"It is."

He didn't ask me to come along. The old times were just that. Old times. Things had changed now. He went over to his stereo system, put in a CD, and turned it on.

Nirvana. Cobain singing from the dead out of the speakers.

Load up on guns and bring your friends

"I like working to music."

"Sean, I can't drink this. Can I get some water instead?"

"Sure. Go help yourself in the kitchen. I need to go clean up in the bathroom anyway."

I went into the kitchen and poured out the scotch. I turned on the faucet, rinsed out my glass a few times and filled it with tap water. That's one of the greatest things about San Francisco. You can drink the water. It's even good for you. It has fluoride in it, so your teeth don't rot out of your mouth.

It's fun to lose and to pretend

I was just about to leave the kitchen when I noticed the stove.

Despite all the modern gadgets in his apartment, Sean still had a gas stove. Gas is a practical choice, especially for San Francisco. You could cook if the electricity went out during an earthquake. You'd starve if you had an electric stove.

Thank goodness for natural gas.

She's over-bored and self-assured

"Timing and opportunity," Sean had said.

And I had both.

CHAPTER
TWENTY-FIVE

WHEN THE MOMENT IS RIGHT and opportunity presents itself, you have to recognize it, seize it, and jump on it with the full weight of your being.

Like at Don's house.

And in Jack's office.

You have to grab on tight, lest it slip through your fingers.

Sean had spiraled out of control. I had no idea whether he was evolving or devolving, but I knew Betty's disappearance would not be easily dismissed by anyone, let alone the police. She wasn't some whore on a corner.

Little old ladies, even nosy, obnoxious ones, garner sympathy from authorities. They represent the helpless in our society. They are upstanding citizens who pay taxes and deserve the attention of the police who are supposed to protect them from predators like Sean.

Not like the young woman who hung around on dark street corners in the middle of the night in a spangled mini skirt and platform stilettos selling her good virtues to the good residents of San Francisco.

Betty's absence would bring the police. Right to Sean's door. She would be one victim too many.

Sean went into a small storage closet and pulled out a handsaw. I watched as he walked into the bathroom with the saw in one hand and a plastic apron in the other.

"There's food in the fridge, Fi. Help yourself," he called out before closing the door behind him.

"Thanks, I will."

I stared at the stove again.

That day Sean set Stephanie's head on fire, he didn't run. He stood there as she screamed, writhing in pain from the flames. He stood there and watched while Sister Maria and Sister Carmen came running to Stephanie's rescue with a fire extinguisher and blankets. But he made no attempts to escape or to avoid punishment.

"I'll have to pay for this, so I might as well enjoy the show," Sean said to me in the chapel.

Sister Maria made him sit in front of the life-sized crucifix while she called the ambulance and police. She wanted Sean to tell Jesus how much he had hurt Him by setting Stephanie ablaze.

I volunteered to watch Sean.

"Don't worry, Sister. You already took away his Zippo. And there are no candles in the chapel."

"Okay, Fiona. But if he tries to hurt you, scream."

Duh.

"Crap, Sean. Now you're in big trouble."

"No worries, Fi. Too young. They'll just send me to juvie."

I started sniffling.

"What's wrong with you, Fi?"

"Who's going to help me thump Jeremy now?"

"No one helped you thump him. You did that on your own."

"Aren't you scared?"

"No."

"But the police, Sean."

"They don't execute kids. And Stephanie's not dead, you know. Can't you hear her screaming?"

Stephanie's cries echoed down the hall all the way from the makeshift infirmary. The ambulance hadn't arrived yet.

"I'm going to miss you, Sean."

"Don't be a crybaby, Fi. I hate crybabies."

So I stopped blubbering. Sean hated weakness. He hated fear and tears. And I didn't want him to hate me.

I knew they wouldn't let Sean off with a dozen Hail Marys or fifty Our Fathers. Not even if he meant every word.

Not even Jesus could change that.

"But we won't get to hang out anymore," I told him.

"Guess you'll have to make new friends."

"Your dad…"

"What's he going to do? Come beat me at juvie?"

Then the police came and took Sean away. And I didn't see him again until I walked into his office to get a hymen.

BUT SEAN WAS TOO OLD for juvie now. He was destined for Death

Row. He didn't seem to care much though.

I poured out my water, washed the glass and placed it on the dish rack after wiping it clean of my prints with a towel. Then I walked over to the stove and stared hard at the dials.

There would be no crappy prison food.

No bright orange jumper.

No sadistic guards.

No unwanted butt sex.

Not for Sean, the love of my life. I would spare him all that cruelty. All that ugliness. All that indignity. Or at least that was what I told myself.

With the lights out, it's less dangerous

Careful not to leave my prints on the knob, I turned on the gas.

Thanks to Darrell and the pencil he shoved up Sean's nose, Sean would never smell a thing.

Good.

And for this gift I feel blessed

The gas hissed out quietly, filling the apartment. I walked around to check the windows. Sean had already closed them and drawn the curtains. He didn't want to disturb the neighbors.

Always thinking of others, Sean was.

Hello, hello, hello, how low?

"Fi?"

Sean poked his head out of the half-closed bathroom door. "Can you check if I have any cigarettes left? Look on the coffee table."

My heart skipped a beat. Cigarettes and gas do not go well together. Fate and karma were colliding through me. Perhaps Sean had been asking for it after all.

"Sean, are you going to smoke? I have asthma."

"Not now. When you leave. After I'm done in here."

"Oh, okay."

I went into the living room. Sure enough, a pack of Dunhills lay on the coffee table. I carefully removed one and slipped it into my pocket.

"Yeah, you've got plenty, Sean."

"Great."

Sean retreated back behind the bathroom door and continued with his work. I looked around at the apartment which was quickly filling up with gas. I coughed twice into my sleeve from the foul smell.

It was time to go.

I looked at the bathroom door and thought about Sean behind it, working diligently. The handsome boy who had prodded me into thumping Jeremy. Who gave me the strength to protect myself from the Jacks and Dons of the world.

For a moment, I wondered what he would look like dead. His eyes, his expression, his cold sneer. Oh well.

And always will until the end

"Don't be a crybaby." That was what Sean had said.

"Sean?" I called his name for the last time.

He cracked the door open again. He had a bit of blood splattered on his cheek, but I didn't say anything. The color suited his complexion.

"Yeah?"

"I need to go back to the office. I have to get a couple of agreements together for Doreen first thing in the morning."

Work.

I never thought it would save my life.

"Okay, see you later, Fi. Let yourself out."

And cut down on the smoking. It'll kill you, Sean.

Oh well, whatever, nevermind

But like he always said, everyone has to die.

CHAPTER
TWENTY-SIX

SIXTY-THREE PERCENT OF FEMALE Chinese mantids' diet consists of male Chinese mantids. She devours him after mating if he's too weak to escape from her clutches. So he can't go and mate with other females and pass on his sissy DNA.

It's a part of the natural selection process. Good old-fashioned Darwinism, sexual evolution. Not to mention the extra nutrition provided.

Someone needs to tell Hello Kitty.

Most people think only black widow spiders eat their mates, but it's not true. Sexual cannibalism is common in many families of spiders, scorpions, and praying mantids. Species that have managed to survive for millions of years. That outlasted the dinosaurs and that will probably still be here when we're gone.

But it's less common among human beings. So when it happens, people freak out a little.

Just look at Dahmer.

He didn't even do it for natural selection or nutrition. He

just wanted his victims to stay with him forever and ever. And everyone called him a sick freak and threw him in jail.

But Dahmer was right.

Consuming the one you love ensures he'll never leave you. You take a little part of him into yourself, making him a part of you. Forever.

Wherever you go, he'll be with you. Walking down the sidewalk, sitting in a tub of dirty bathwater, working in an office fifteen hours a day. More portable than an iPod Nano, and even better.

Portability is more important than ever now. The airlines are charging fifteen to twenty-five dollars for each piece of checked luggage. A girl's gotta travel light. Can't get weighed down in the modern world. Can't risk leaving something behind on the baggage carousel. Or on a sailboat. Or on a schoolyard. Ever.

Nothing gets left behind. That's all Dahmer wanted to avoid. Being left behind.

Oh well.

The next morning, I left home an hour earlier than usual, citing an early morning meeting. But instead, I went to Walgreen's, where you can get anything from condoms to ear medicine to wine bottle openers, all at a low, reasonable price. I purchased a ninety-nine-cent lighter, one of those cheap ones stocked next to the cash register.

Then I walked over to the remains of Sean's apartment on Russian Hill. I had heard the fire engines screaming last night towards Sean's place. I smelled the smoke, heard the boom, turned over and went to sleep.

But now I stood on the sidewalk in front of the apartment building, looking up at the large, gaping black hole which used to be his living room window. Bits of charred debris littered the ground, along with glass, plaster, and evidence of the firefighters' efforts of rescue.

I pulled out my cheap lighter and the Dunhill cigarette I took from Sean from my coat pocket. And lit it.

I put the cigarette to my lips and inhaled. The hot, rich smoke burned my throat, making me cough violently. But undaunted, I tried it again. It was better the second time and the third. Asthma be damned. Everyone has to die.

I stood there looking up at the remains of Sean's apartment, smoking Sean's cigarette and recalling the conversation we had on *The Countess* that day we sailed to Angel Island. I thought about what he had said about his ashes and what he wanted. And then I took a deep breath, telling myself that that was what Sean would have wanted. That's what people always tell themselves.

And then I took another.

And another.

I was inhaling Sean's ashes, essence, spirit, whatever was left of him in the air around me. It was better than consuming his flesh, his genitals, his body parts. Lower risk of contracting a disease. No risk of someone calling me a freak.

A mulatto, an albino

But it's very much the same thing, whether it goes through the nose or the mouth. All those little tiny particles, like mini ticks and fleas.

A mosquito, my libido

With my lungs full of Sean, I went to work.

"Good morning, Doreen."

And it truly was a good morning.

"Fiona, have you been smoking?"

"No, Doreen, I don't smoke. But I was walking down the street behind someone who was puffing away."

"How inconsiderate. I hope you said something."

"Nah, you never know. He could be one of those nutters who'll punch you in the face for saying something."

"True."

Doreen knew the City too.

I turned on my computer, checking the local news online. I didn't even have to search for the story. It was under the Breaking News section.

Local Surgeon Killed in Gas Explosion: Dr. Sean Killroy, 29, a prominent plastic surgeon of San Francisco, died yesterday evening in an explosion at his Russian Hill apartment. Investigators believe Killroy accidentally set off the explosion when he struck a match to light a cigarette, unaware that his apartment had a gas leak. The explosion also claimed the life of Killroy's neighbor, Betty Mulroney, 86, who was found in Killroy's apartment. Authorities believe the two victims had been friends…

Betty and Sean. Friends. How lovely. More newspaper half-truths.

Here we are now, entertain us

A professional picture of Sean smiling in a white doctor's coat with a stethoscope around his neck accompanied the article, which continued with a discussion of the dangers of smoking, the impact tobacco has on daily life, and how this tragedy could have been avoided if Dr. Killroy, who was a doctor and should have known better, had quit smoking.

Guess Sean should have heeded the warning on cigarette packages:

SURGEON GENERAL'S WARNING: Quitting Smoking Now Greatly Reduces Serious Risks to Your Health

That was certainly true in his case.

But Sean had gotten part of his wish.

He had wanted to be cremated. The explosion certainly took care of that, but too bad Betty hadn't been alive to choke on his ashes. At least the rest of his neighbors would.

At least, I did. Just like a good little Chinese mantis.

I considered the portrait of the Blood Countess decorating my computer desktop. So outdated. By over four hundred years. It was time for an upgrade. Time to go fresh, young, modern.

I clicked on Sean's picture from the article and set it as my desktop background. Much better.

"Who's that?" someone would eventually ask.

"The love of my life," I would tell them.

"Lucky you."

Yes, that's what someone would say.

Sean definitely looked better than the Blood Countess. All that blood did absolutely nothing for the woman. She still died in the end, just like everyone else. What a psycho bitch.

Sean smiled at me from my desktop. Reminding me to give it to Doreen, if she asked for it.

Reminding me I didn't need a hymen.

Reminding me I could handle the Dons and Freddies of the

world. Or any other boy my father threw at me.

A denial

I have no idea why Cobain screams "a denial" a gazillion times at the end of "Smells Like Teen Spirit". No one does, actually. That's the great thing about the song. No one really gets it.

So you can pretend he's saying anything you want.

It sounds like he's mumbling "bloody liar" to me. It really does. Listen to it. But then again, Weird Al Yankovic made a good case in his video parody of Nirvana that Cobain was screaming "Sayonara."

Oh, what the hell.

Cobain was cooked to the gills on drugs. If anything, you have to give him a break and blame the drugs.

So yeah, I'll cook for you.

Bloody liar

I'll wash your clothes.

Bloody liar

I'll have your two and a half brats.

Bloody liar

And suck your cock. Just like a good Hello Kitty.

Bloody liar

Hi, I'm Fiona Yu.

Sayonara

And it's so very nice to meet you.

Whatever.

THE END

www.vintage-books.co.uk